A DEADLY REUNION

A DEADLY
REUNION

•

MARILYN PRATHER

AVALON BOOKS
THOMAS BOUREGY AND COMPANY, INC.
401 LAFAYETTE STREET
NEW YORK, NEW YORK 10003

PRINTED IN THE UNITED STATES OF AMERICA
ON ACID-FREE PAPER
BY HADDON CRAFTSMEN, SCRANTON, PENNSYLVANIA

To
LaDeane, Marcie, and Ryan Fenton
and
Michele Rothrock
and
Bob and Carol West,
my friends and inspiration

Chapter One

"So, what's this, Rach? *The Neillson High Windjammer?*"

Rachel Anders smiled at the questioning look on her best friend's face. "My high school yearbook, Meg. Senior year."

"Of course." Meg Simms ran her hand over the blue-and-white cover. "Preparing for the big night." She flashed Rachel a grin. "May I take a peek?"

Rachel took hold of Meg's arm. "You'd told me you were in a rush. Are you showing a house?" She began to lead Meg away from the table where the yearbook lay open.

Meg shook her head.

"No! It's Wednesday," Rachel corrected herself. "That means pizza and watching football with Phil."

"Not quite. Six months ago it was football. Now it's baseball," Meg said in gentle retort. "But the pizza's the same. Pepperoni," she added with a laugh.

Rachel could remember a time when she'd been on a tight schedule too. Only instead of pizza and sports, she had been treated to prime rib and dancing afterwards.

"If you won't let me look at your yearbook, then show me the dress you bought for the reunion. You do want my esteemed opinion, don't you?"

Rachel smiled. "I do." But the word "reunion" caused a knot of uncertainty to settle in her stomach as the two friends crossed into the bedroom of Rachel's apartment.

Meg sat down on the edge of the bed while Rachel got the dress in question from the closet and hurried into the bathroom to change. Emerging with the dress on, Rachel did a slow pirouette in front of the bed. "What's the verdict?" she asked a little apprehensively.

Meg's reply was a low whistle that made Rachel giggle. "It's perfect, Rach. Absolutely, totally perfect. And the teal color matches your eyes."

Relieved at her friend's pronouncement, Rachel examined the dress, and herself, in the mirror. "You really think the color's good for me?"

"Fantastic. With that blond hair and porcelain complexion you'll be the envy of every woman there. I guarantee it."

Teal eyes, porcelain complexion? Rachel frowned at her image. Meg had a way with words, but Rachel couldn't imagine herself making that much of an impression on her former classmates. She thought of one person in particular. Jeff Martin—a former classmate, yes, but he had been so much more than that. . . .

Meg put her hand on Rachel's arm. "Don't worry. Maybe Jeff won't show. And even if he does, you'll be having such a good time you won't care."

Meg knew the reason for Rachel's discomfort; that was one thing Rachel couldn't hide from her friend. Rachel sighed. "I hope you're right." A vivid memory from the past took over her mind. She could see herself and Jeff at the senior prom. The old gym had been transformed, as if by magic, into a lovely garden complete with waterfall.

The dance had been a decade ago, but the intoxicating scent of lilacs tickled her nostrils as if the flowers were blooming in her bedroom. And she could hear the band too, playing an achingly romantic song, as Jeff held her in his arms. When the song had ended that night, he'd kissed her softly and sweetly. But the tenderness of the moment was forever tarnished by a far more bitter memory.

"Rach?"

"I—" Rachel shook her head. "I was just thinking of how it used to be." She put on a brave smile. 'I'm okay." Meg looked skeptical. "I'll *be* okay," she amended. She couldn't fool Meg; she'd told her too much about Jeff's charming ways—and his not-so-charming darker side.

"I remember when I was dating Brian." Meg's arm came around Rachel's shoulder. "The cheerleader and the quarterback. So typical." Meg laughed, but her eyes reflected concern for her friend.

"I know," Rachel said quietly. It had been very different with her and Jeff. They'd been anything but a typical couple. She'd been president of the debate club; he'd earned the nickname "the Doctor" after showing a penchant for examining dead frogs and other creatures in zoology class their sophomore year.

Cutting open frogs and dull-eyed fish had made Rachel squeamish. The smell of formaldehyde had left her dizzy. But she'd never let on, not when Jeff's ambitions included premed at Yale. The idea that she would one day be married to a physician had pleased her too much.

Jeff's ambitions *had* been realized, only not in the way she, or anyone else, had anticipated.

"I'm sorry," Meg was saying. "I didn't mean to trivialize your relationship with Jeff. Brian and I were an item for a while, but it soon cooled off. You and Jeff were serious."

Rachel had to agree with that. Engaged to be married at twenty had definitely seemed serious.

"When was the last time you saw him, Rach?"

Rachel closed her eyes briefly. "Seven months ago." She recalled the day, the time, every detail, though she was loath to admit it. "At the Twelfth Street Mall, in front of Berman's Department Store." He'd sported a wool tweed jacket and tan slacks. The only change she had noticed in him was that he wore his dark hair longer than she'd remembered it. His sarcastic smile was the same. And his eyes. Those brooding eyes had met hers with such a look of possessiveness that she'd shivered and turned away.

"He probably has a girlfriend, or several," Meg offered. "Maybe he's even married."

"I don't think so, Meg. I would have seen it in the paper." Since shortly after their breakup she'd had an almost obsessive habit of checking the engagement and wedding columns in the newspaper. It reminded her of the way some people checked the obituaries.

"Promise me something, Rach."

"What?"

Meg's expression was earnest. "Promise that between now and Saturday night, you'll think only good thoughts. Consider the friends you just can't wait to see again. Everything's going to turn out fine. I can feel it."

Rachel had to smile at Meg's optimism. "I'll try," she said at last.

Meg glanced at her watch. "I'm sorry, Rach, but I've got to run."

Rachel understood, but a part of her felt disappointed. She wished Meg was able to stay and talk; she could use more bolstering. "I'll walk you to the door," she offered. "Can you stop by the store tomorrow?"

"Anything interesting come in?"

"Only a huge consignment from Lucy Benson."

Meg's eyebrows shot up. "The dentist's wife?" She paused at the front door. "I have a seminar tomorrow and Friday. How to successfully close a sale." Meg made a face. "Boring, but very necessary for me to attend."

"And you're visiting a friend in Detroit over the weekend." This time Rachel gave Meg a reassuring squeeze. "Don't worry. I'll stash all of Lucy's goodies in the storeroom. No one else will see a thread of her designer dresses before you. How about Monday after work?"

"Do you really think I'm that much of a clothes-horse?" Meg teased.

"Yes."

They both laughed. "Well, if you want the truth, I can't wait to get a report on the reunion, Rach."

"I'll tell you every awful detail, until you beg me to quit." After a hug, Rachel watched Meg hurry off toward the elevator.

"Say hi to Phil for me," Rachel called. Though she was smiling, her spirits had already begun to droop and doubts about the wisdom of attending her tenth high school reunion plagued her again.

Rachel stood in front of the wall-length mirror in the ladies' lounge of St. Paul's newest hotel, the Quincy Inn. She had to concede the reunion committee had gone all out, renting one of the inn's large ballrooms instead of choosing the more practical, if gritty, Neillson High gym. She was just as glad; the gym might have provoked a storm of unwanted memories guaranteed to make her miserable.

By contrast, the ballroom was elegantly appointed, with brass and glass chandeliers and gilded white wall paper. And the lounge was just as plush; a cozy-looking divan had been set against the wall. She decided it might come in handy later if things got too tense.

Nothing of consequence had happened yet, Rachel told herself. She'd been at the reunion for over an hour, and wasn't she having a good time? She was, but the queasiness that had been her companion ever since she'd entered the hotel served to temper her enthusiasm—even if the person who'd caused it hadn't put in an appearance.

At least as far as she could tell, Jeff wasn't in attendance. She prayed Meg had guessed right and that he wouldn't come at all.

Leaning close to the mirror, she made a study of her hair and makeup. Her eyes did look sort of teal with the dress, although their usual color was a pale blue. Her blond hair was only a slightly darker shade than it had been a decade ago, but now she wore it in a sleeker, chin-length style rather than long and wavy. It suited her well, friends told her.

"Did you *see* Robby Ransom?"

"Rob. It's Rob now, Kerrie."

"Who cares? Rob, Robby—I say he's gorgeous. And before the night's over, he'll be mine."

Rachel peeked through lowered lashes at the women who had come into the lounge. One of them, a short woman with straight black hair, she didn't recognize. The other she knew immediately. Kerrie Bowles, man chaser and notorious flirt, was the one who'd boldly declared her intentions toward Rob Ransom, another classmate.

Kerrie was dressed in a short, red leather skirt and matching fringed vest. It was the kind of outfit only she could get by with, Rachel thought with a twinge of envy.

She and Kerrie had never been close friends in school. To say they'd been cordial to each other would have been an exaggeration.

Kerrie ignored Rachel, continuing the conversation about Rob with her friend. "Can you believe that luscious piece of manhood is real?"

Rachel rolled her eyes at the statement, grateful Kerrie wasn't paying any attention to her. She remembered Rob Ransom as an obnoxious kid, the class clown. The fact that he'd also been skinny and given to tripping over his own feet had heightened his comedic value. Yet it hadn't won him the popularity, or respect, he'd sought.

If Kerrie and her friend were right, it sounded like Rob's fortunes had changed. Rachel was sure she'd soon find out. According to the program booklet she'd been handed at the door, Rob was scheduled to emcee the evening.

"Rachel? Rachel Anders?"

Rachel turned at the sound of her name, surprised that Kerrie must have noticed her after all. But it wasn't Kerrie who had spoken. Her eyes met those of a very attractive woman whose face looked hauntingly familiar. Yet she couldn't place it.

The woman tilted her head and frowned. "Rachel?" She took a tentative step forward.

Something in the way the woman moved stirred a memory in Rachel. "Mickey? Is it *really* Mickey?"

"You didn't recognize me, did you?" The words were mildly accusing.

Rachel's mouth hung open in astonishment. "No," she replied honestly. "No, I didn't." Then she threw her arms around Mickey.

Michaela Franklin had been part of Rachel's circle of close friends, though always on the fringes. Her weight problem had been the reason. Rachel knew it; everyone knew it. They had tried to make Mickey feel accepted. Rachel had never been sure they'd succeeded.

When all of the others had talked excitedly about their boyfriends, Mickey had kept silent. She didn't have a boyfriend. As far as Rachel knew, through high school Mickey had never had a date. She never went to dances, never went bowling or skiing or skating on Gramercy Pond like everyone else. She did accompany them to Louie's Pizza for a super supreme with double cheese, or to the Creamery for a hot-fudge sundae.

Over time Rachel had come to see herself as Mickey's advocate, coming to her friend's defense when others made cruel jokes about Mickey's weight. It had never occurred to Rachel whether Mickey would rather stand up for herself. Not until this moment.

No doubt the reason it suddenly came to her mind was because the Mickey standing in front of her bore virtually no resemblance to the "old" Mickey. For a moment Rachel just stared, unable to stop herself. Finally she found her voice. "You look fabulous, Mickey." The declaration sounded more like it came from a frog.

It was obvious that Mickey no longer needed someone to protect her, unless it would be from the hordes of eager males who no doubt clamored to take her out. She had shed every ounce of her excess weight and the red, clingy dress she wore did nothing to hide her fantastic figure.

Mickey's full mouth curved into a brief smile, but her dark eyes held a guarded expression. "You look great too, Rachel," she said coolly. "Have you seen the others yet?" Mickey glanced around the lounge, but didn't greet Kerrie Bowles and her companion who were by now staring at her too.

Kerrie's reaction gave Rachel a rush of satisfaction, though she didn't let on. "Sue's in the ballroom," she replied to Mickey's question. "Did you just get here?"

Mickey nodded. Her eyes traveled over Rachel for a moment. They landed on Rachel's left hand. "What? No ring?" she asked, inspecting the naked third finger. "I thought you and Jeff would be married."

Warmth flooded Rachel's face; she prayed Kerrie hadn't overheard, though she asked herself what difference it made. Shaking her head mutely, Rachel said, "Let's go find Sue. Diane should be with her." She ignored Mickey's puzzled look, taking her by the hand to pull her from the lounge.

The cool air in the corridor hit Rachel's face. It felt good after the stuffy atmosphere of the lounge.

The ballroom was crowded, but when they got near, Rachel saw Sue standing just inside. Head back, long brown hair flowing over her shoulders, Sue was laughing. She'd always had a wicked sense of humor, Rachel remembered with a smile.

"There's Diane!"

Rachel followed Mickey's outstretched arm. Diane was only yards from Sue. Rachel let go of Mickey's hand and hurried to greet Diane.

Diane's arms came around her, enveloping her. No weight loss on Diane's part. She was still slightly plump. She still had bright red hair. And she still glowed.

That was the only word to describe the vibrant quality about Diane that had always drawn people to her, even as a somewhat clumsy sixteen-year-old.

"Oh, Rachel!" Diane hugged her tighter until she could hardly breathe.

In the background, Rachel heard Sue call Mickey's name and she caught a glimpse of them embracing. Then Diane turned to stare at Mickey.

"No! Mickey!" Diane released Rachel and ran to hug Mickey. "You look beautiful!"

Mickey's face was flushed—whether it was pride or self-consciousness, Rachel wasn't sure.

Sue suggested the four of them circulate around the ballroom. As they did, she turned to Diane. "As I'd started to ask, is it Melnick or—"

"Braverman," Diane interrupted. "My husband's name is Derek Braverman. He couldn't come, I'm afraid. He's tied up in a conference back in New York. Derek's a stockbroker," she added breathlessly.

Rachel hoped her surprise didn't show. Though she and Diane had lost contact with each other over the years, the last she'd heard Diane had declared her life belonged to the Peace Corps. It was hard to imagine she'd dedicated herself instead to living in the fast track.

"We met in Panama," Diane added, giving Rachel's arm a squeeze. "One intensely gorgeous summer night. There was a full moon over Panama Bay."

"It must have been very romantic." Rachel forced herself to smile, but the image conjured up in her mind made her heart contract wildly.

Diane's eyes grew wide. "Definitely romantic." She averted her gaze, then abruptly switched topics. Looking around the ballroom, she asked, "Where's Jeff?"

It was what Rachel had dreaded—and feared being asked over and over. She followed Diane's gaze, as if she were hunting for him too. The room was packed with people; none of the faces she saw was Jeff's. Yet she couldn't form an answer to Diane's question.

Sue suddenly put herself between Rachel and Diane. "I'm starved. Aren't you, Rachel?" Not waiting for a reply, she said, "The buffet table's only open until eight-thirty. Then we have the privilege of allowing a muscled Rob Ransom to amuse us—if you want to call what he does amusing."

Rachel barely heard Sue's words, but she could have kissed her for the timely intervention. Of the three friends, Sue was the one she'd kept in closest touch with, mostly by phone. Though months passed between the times they actually saw each other, Rachel figured that, next to Meg, Sue probably knew the most about her personal life.

"Have you seen Rob yet?" Rachel directed her question at Sue.

"No. I guess even someone who likes attention as much as Rob can get lost in a crowd of three hundred people. I've heard rumors about him though," she added, grinning.

"What rumors?" Diane put in, apparently dropping the subject of Jeff Martin for the present.

"Rob Ransom's a hunk," Mickey said dryly.

"Then you've seen him."

"Negative," Mickey replied.

Rachel had to laugh at the expression on Mickey's face, if for no other reason. Her laughter died as soon as she put her arm around Sue. The bony protuberance of Sue's shoulder blade startled Rachel. Sue had always been lithe and very conscious of her weight. But feeling the evidence of just how thin she was made Rachel wonder if her friend's obsession with dieting had gone too far. Could it be that Sue was anorexic?

Rachel's sense of alarm was pushed aside when she realized that Mickey had fallen behind. That was an old habit of Mickey's. But there was no longer any reason why she should feel the need to stay in the shadows.

Rachel decided it was time for that to change too. "Come on, Mickey. You go first." She gave Mickey a slight push in the direction of the buffet table. Sue and Diane lined up behind her.

"Maybe you'll bump into Rob." Sue directed her comment at Mickey.

Mickey grimaced as Sue began to help herself from a huge icy bowl filled with cocktail shrimp. "You'll render him speechless. Besides, there're worse things than meeting the man of your dreams over Caesar salad."

"Rob isn't the man of my dreams," Mickey said stonily.

Though Rachel felt no particular warmth toward Rob, she wondered at Mickey's response. Could it be that Mickey was curious about Rob, but didn't want her friends to know?

Diane touched Mickey's arm. "I think you'll meet someone special tonight." Her tone of voice was a bit condescending.

Rachel shot her a look. "I'm sure there's already someone special in Mickey's life," she quickly interceded.

"There's not." Mickey's short reply added to Rachel's surprise, but her face was turned away so that Rachel couldn't see her expression.

As she piled shrimp on her own plate, Rachel prayed that the subject of Mickey's love life, as well as her own, would be put to rest. But she had to admit she was curious about Sue's.

After they'd loaded their plates with food, Sue led the group to one of the tables set along a wall of the ballroom.

They did more talking than eating as they caught up on one another's activities. Diane and Mickey were pleased to learn that Rachel had opened her own consignment boutique.

"What do you call it?" Mickey asked, spearing a piece of fresh pineapple on her plate.

"Cabbage Rose's."

Mickey's fork stopped halfway to her mouth. "Cabbage Rose?"

"That's the name of a doll," Sue explained, grinning as she picked at her salad.

Rachel was distracted for a moment, watching Sue toy with her food. She was certain her friend hadn't eaten more than two bites from her heaped-up plate. She said finally, "Cabbage Rose is a special doll. She belonged to my great-grandmother. When Mom and Dad moved to San Francisco two years ago, Mom entrusted Cabbage Rose to me." *Along with a sizable loan to open the store of my dreams,* she might have added. "Cabbage Rose sits in the window and greets customers."

"A watch doll," Diane quipped, and everyone broke up laughing.

"That's great," Mickey said. "Your own business."

"What about you, Mickey?"

"Yes, tell us," Rachel added to Diane's question, anxious to draw attention away from herself. "A runway model for Bermans?"

Mickey took her time placing her fork beside her plate. "Parking meter attendant for the city of St. Paul," she replied in a monotone.

"Really?" Diane looked incredulous.

"Really." Mickey said it with a dose of sarcasm that squelched any further questions.

Diane seemed bent on patronizing Mickey and it irritated Rachel, much as she was fond of Diane. Those protective instincts rose in her breast, but she kept her mouth shut.

"Well, before you ask," Sue said lightly, "I'm assistant manager of the Europa Spa on Kelly Boulevard."

Though Rachel murmured her approval along with the others, she felt that sense of alarm again. Did Sue lead exercise classes all day in an attempt to shake off even more weight?

"I'm an administrative assistant to a criminal lawyer *and* a domestic engineer," Diane said with a proud smile.

"Any little junior engineers?" That came from Sue.

"Not yet, but Derek and I are working on it."

While the remark drew giggles, Rachel thought she

saw sadness in Sue's eyes. She had a suspicion she knew why.

"Has anyone seen Todd Andrews yet?"

Sue's question confirmed the suspicion. They hadn't discussed the subject lately, but through most of high school, Sue'd had a thing for Todd. More than a crush—unrequited love. Never mind that Todd had been deeply involved with a petite, pretty girl named Stacey Trabeck.

It had hardly been a shock to hear Sue's confession of love for Todd. Any girl in school could have fallen for him, Rachel supposed. Even as young as fifteen, he had been pretty spectacular. Blond hair, wavy and thick, similar to her own. And blue eyes—but a much darker, moodier shade than hers.

Once, a girl new to Neillson High had asked Rachel if she and Todd were twins. Though she'd considered the idea funny, she had felt flattered too. She and Todd had known each other since first grade. In classes where the teacher favored alphabetical seating, Todd had always sat at the desk right behind hers.

Maybe he'd changed since high school and neither she nor Sue would recognize him. She thought of several male classmates she'd seen that evening who had developed paunches or were going bald. She smiled to herself; it was impossible to imagine Todd with a paunch or without hair.

"He's married, isn't he?"

Diane's question brought Rachel out of her introspection. "I think so," she said carefully, darting a glance at Sue.

Sue's eyes met hers and held them. "Divorced, I believe." She pushed her plate aside, the food hardly touched.

Rachel was surprised by the news. Everyone had taken for granted that someday Todd and Stacey would marry. But there had been times, Rachel recalled, when Todd had looked unhappy, times when Stacey had acted bossy with him. Or had that just been her imagination?

"Do you remember the time Todd dipped your braid in a jar of tempera paint?"

Diane's question was directed at Rachel. "Yes," she acknowledged, smiling at the memory despite her disturbed feelings over the news of Todd and Stacey's divorce. "Todd did worse than that too."

He had been a tease, had loved playing practical jokes on her. But she'd known his intent hadn't been malicious; he'd only wanted to razz her.

"He liked you, Rachel."

The remark came from Mickey and she said it with a straight face.

"Of course, he liked me," Rachel retorted. "As a friend," she added.

"No," Mickey insisted. "He *liked* you, *not* as a friend."

"You mean a crush?" Diane put in. Her eyes lit up with interest.

Rachel raised her hands in a defensive gesture. "Come on! No way, Mickey." But Mickey's glaring look told Rachel she was serious. It made Rachel uncomfortable. What could Sue be thinking? Looking at Sue under lowered lashes told her nothing. Sue's face was expressionless; was it only a cover-up for her anger?

Rachel had no more time to consider the matter as Rob Ransom's voice suddenly boomed over the loudspeaker.

"May I have your attention please?" he repeated.

"You've got it, whether we like it or not," Mickey muttered.

Rachel smiled at Mickey; it wasn't returned. With a shrug, Rachel looked toward the dais that had been set up in the middle of the room.

At least the rumors about Rob were all true. He stood

in front of the microphone, clad in a light-blue blazer that somehow managed to show off his muscles instead of hiding them. He *was* a hunk, and a good half of the female population in the room went crazy, whistling and calling his name.

Rachel stole a peek at Mickey; she appeared totally disgusted. Rachel wondered why she'd taken such an interest in Mickey's opinion of the man when it was obvious he was as obnoxious as he was handsome.

His ego no doubt inflated to Mt. McKinley proportions, "Mr. Charm" fired off several absurdly corny jokes. The audience howled with laughter, even Rachel, though she would have been embarrassed to admit it. Inspired, he tossed off a few more before settling down to the serious business of the evening, introducing special guests.

First came Darwin Mears, Neillson High's dour chemistry teacher. He didn't look amused when Rob declared that chemistry had been his favorite class. If Rachel's memory was right, Rob Ransom had squeaked through the course with a D.

Rob then called Betsy Bolton, Neillson High's librarian, to the dais. Betsy ducked her head demurely at the round of applause from the audience, but not before Rob planted an enthusiastic kiss on her cheek.

A number of awards followed. Rob held up a plastic statuette. "This, um, lovely likeness of 'The Thinker' goes to Kevin McClure." The crowd applauded wildly.

"Kevin's a producer in Hollywood," Sue whispered. "Maybe Rob's angling for a contract." Mickey ignored the remark; Rachel nodded in agreement.

A "chrome dome" award went to Drew Potts.

"I can't imagine it. He used to have this much hair." Diane held her hands out from her head. The remark brought a small smile to Mickey's lips.

The "cheaper by the dozen" award was bestowed on a couple who had an astounding six children.

It was Rachel's turn to make a comment. "Wow! What else do they do?"

"Any *grandchildren?*" Rob exaggerated the word, leaning into the mike. His eyes scanned the room. The crowd's response was a smattering of catcalls.

Rob shrugged. "Hey, you know something I don't?" He shielded his eyes. "Jeff and Rachel? Where are the Martins?"

At the sound of her name, Rachel froze. Vaguely, she heard Mickey say, "The man's insufferable." A hand took hold of hers. It was Diane's.

"Yoo-hoo, Martins! Any grandkids?"

The room fell silent and Rachel sensed everyone's eyes on her. She stared straight ahead until, after what seemed an eternity, Rob went on to the next award.

"Thank you," she whispered to her friends.

"It's okay. I don't think anyone saw you." The remark was Sue's and though Rachel doubted it was true, she was grateful for the show of support.

Moments later, Rob announced that the band would be setting up on the portable stage that had just been wheeled into the ballroom.

"And the rest of the night, my fellow classmates, is for wining, dining, and dancing." He made an elaborate bow. "Don't forget to pick up your reunion souvenir books at the registration table." He seemed about to leave when he turned back to the microphone. In a husky, seductive voice, he said, "Save me a dance, Mickey."

Rachel gasped; she was sure Sue and Diane did too.

But not Mickey. Under her breath, she pronounced, "That creep."

Rachel believed again that her friend's remark might be a cover-up. And she had to wonder if Rob had any clue how much Mickey had changed. Secretly, she felt a guilty pleasure in his request. Kerrie Bowles was aware of Mickey's transformation; she had to be more than a little worried that Rob would soon find out for himself— and like what he saw.

"Why don't we go mingle?" The suggestion was Diane's.

When neither Rachel nor Mickey responded, Sue urged, "I think it would do you both good."

"Okay," Mickey said at last.

Rachel's reply was to put on a stoic smile and get up from her chair. To her relief, she found the mingling was not so bad. She ran into several people she'd hoped to see, not the least of whom was her former senior year debating partner. He introduced Rachel to his wife, explaining they had met through the debate club at the university they'd both attended.

In the background, the band tuned up their instruments. Then the lead singer introduced the band's first number, and Rachel's debating partner excused himself and his wife. Rachel watched as they moved onto the dance floor.

Scanning the crowd, she spotted Sue and headed her way. But she came up short when she spied Kerrie Bowles in the midst of the group of people that included Sue and Diane. She looked and saw Mickey standing a little apart from the others.

Rachel must have caught Diane's eye. Diane took Sue's arm, steering her Rachel's way; Mickey followed.

"Rachel, did you know Kerrie Bowles has been modeling for Bloomingdale's in New York?" The question wa Sue's.

"No. Somehow I'm not surprised."

"And she thinks she's in love with—" Sue stopped mid-sentence, her eyes growing large.

Rachel turned to discover what had caused Sue's awed expression. She froze when she felt a hand on her shoulder and heard a very masculine voice ask, ''May I have this dance?''

Chapter Two

Rachel finally got her muscles to move. Looking up, she found herself staring into the tanned face of Todd Andrews. No wonder Sue had been rendered speechless. The passing of a decade had done nothing to diminish Todd's good looks; no paunch or bald pate there.

He wore a navy-blue sports coat and white slacks, and if "hunk" was the word that fit Rob Ransom's toned body, Rachel couldn't think of one to describe Todd's. Magnificent, maybe?

"Unless your husband would mind." Todd smiled. His eyes left hers to scan the room, but soon returned.

"I—" Talk about tongue-tied. Rachel suddenly felt warm. She was sure her reaction to Todd was caused by Mickey's recent proclamation—that, and her strong suspicion that Sue still cared for Todd. *Just friends, old friends,* Rachel reminded herself. *That's all Todd and I are.*

Apparently her silence hadn't put him off. His smile

became a full-fledged grin, showing off his flawlessly even teeth. "Of course, I could just stick gum on your chair," he went on. "Only you don't look like you're about to sit down."

Rachel smiled wanly, shifting her eyes for a second to peer at Sue. As she might have guessed, Sue was still gaping at Todd, but then so were Diane and Mickey, she noted. "All right," she said at last. "One dance."

"One," he agreed. Briefly, he acknowledged Sue, Diane, and Mickey before he took her hand to lead her onto the dance floor.

Surely he would ask each of them for a dance too, Rachel told herself. To Diane she mouthed a "Be back soon," ducking her head Betsy Bolton-style when she passed Sue.

The band started a new number, a slow one. Rachel felt Todd's arm come around her waist. "I've been watching you all evening," he said.

The revelation took her by surprise. "You have?"

"Uh-huh." He gazed down at her, but didn't elaborate.

At first they danced a bit awkwardly and Rachel chided herself for her nervousness. She soon discovered Todd was a very good dancer. It wasn't long before she relaxed in his arms, easily following his steps.

"Jeff's not with you, is he, Rachel?"

The directness of the question took her by surprise. Her muscles bunched again. "No." She paused. "And Stacey's not with you, is she?"

It was Todd's turn to stiffen. He moved away from her almost imperceptibly, but only for a second. "We've been divorced for three years now. Stacey left me. She found someone else."

"I'm sorry."

He shook his head. "Me, too, but I've accepted it and I'm . . . okay now."

Rachel wondered if it was true. Her eyes met his, searching them. She thought she saw a shadow of vulnerability in the dark blue depths.

"How about you, Rachel? Are you okay?" Todd's hold on her tightened a bit.

"Jeff and I were engaged. It's been a couple of years since we broke up."

Todd studied her face as she'd studied his.

"Where are you living?" It wasn't quite the question she wanted to ask.

"Here, in St. Paul."

"Really?"

"Really." He looked pleased.

Rachel liked that. It wasn't all she liked. There was the feeling of warmth where his hand surrounded hers, the slight pressure of his arm at her waist.

"I just moved back to town," he went on, guiding her to the side of the room as the song ended. "From Seattle."

"What brought you back?"

"I was hoping to see you." Again his face wore an intent expression as he gazed down at her. "I'm a developer and I got an offer from the Silverthorne Company, one I couldn't refuse."

She recognized the company name immediately. Silverthorne was one of the largest real estate firms in the Twin Cities—and in recent years had been at the center of more than one controversy. "That's great," she said at last, hoping she sounded sincere. She was happy for Todd, for any career advancement that came his way. But she couldn't help feeling a little uncomfortable.

She was certain Todd was scrupulously honest. He'd been an honor-roll student through high school, a born leader and genuinely nice guy. She couldn't believe he would change, and she hoped he wouldn't be disappointed in his career move.

"What about you? Where do you live, Rachel?" He seemed eager to know.

"In St. Paul too. I guess you could say I never left home." She noted his appreciative smile. "I own a clothing boutique."

"I'd always believed you had a head for business. I'd like to see your store sometime. What do you call it?"

"Cabbage Rose's." She said it with relish; his smile widened.

The band struck up another number. Before Rachel knew what was happening, Todd had asked her for "just one more" dance and she'd said yes.

As they swayed to the music, Rachel's eyes furtively swept the room, searching for a thin woman with long, dark hair. When she didn't see Sue, she felt relieved and guilty at the same time.

And though she was tempted to ask Todd if he might request a dance of Sue, she was also aware of how neatly she fit in his arms, how natural it felt to be with him. In her high heels, she came just to his chin.

Circling the floor, they passed other couples they recognized. As greetings were exchanged, Rachel noted the looks of surprise on some of her former classmates' faces. She hated to contemplate what gossip might spread through the ballroom before the night was over.

When the song ended, Todd kept his arm at her waist until the lead vocalist for the band took the microphone to announce that he would be taking requests. Then he launched into a soulfully romantic tune.

"That's too good to pass up, don't you think?" Todd said close to her ear.

What could she do but agree, though her conscience gave her another stab. Hesitating, she asked, "Todd, I was wondering if maybe . . . you would ask Sue for a dance tonight? I'm sure she'd enjoy that."

Todd gave her a questioning look. "Are you trying to ditch me, Rachel?"

The way he was holding her right now told her he was only teasing. "No." She smiled. "It's just that Sue's been, well, down lately. I thought a dance with you would cheer her up."

"I'll ask her. But just one." His playful reminder of what she'd said several dances ago made Rachel giggle. She rested her cheek against the cool cloth of his blazer, content for the moment just to be held by him. Everything took on a soft, fuzzy appearance.

Then a familiar face came across her line of vision and everything jolted back into focus. She let out a small gasp of surprise.

Jeff Martin stood nearby, on the fringes of a large crowd of people. He was staring at her in an unnerving way that sent a shiver up her spine.

Rachel couldn't keep from staring back. Jeff's face was expressionless. There wasn't a flicker of recognition disturbing the sharp features. He could have been staring through her, not at her.

She looked away first, feeling cold despite the warmth of Todd's presence.

"What's wrong?"

Todd had noticed. Her head jerked up; her eyes met his. "I just saw Jeff."

The pressure of Todd's hand at her waist increased, though he said nothing. She mumbled that she was fine, feeling a bit foolish.

But he deftly turned her in the opposite direction, effectively blocking out any sight of Jeff. Yet she still felt Jeff's eyes on her, probing, even when Todd took her back to where her friends waited.

"Stay here," Todd whispered to her just before he turned to Sue.

She missed Sue's reaction to Todd's request, but she

watched as Sue followed him onto the dance floor. Then a voice distracted Rachel. It was Rob Ransom's and he was asking Mickey to dance.

Rachel held her breath until she heard Mickey's response. Though Mickey didn't appear thrilled at the opportunity, Rachel still believed her friend was masking her true feelings. Mickey had been hurt so many times in high school. Hadn't Rob himself been among those who'd taunted Mickey about her weight?

Rachel smiled to herself. No doubt Rob had seen the "new" Mickey earlier and that's why he'd made the suggestive remark from the dais for everyone to hear. But where was Kerrie Bowles?

Not far, as it happened. Rachel spotted Kerrie and her friend; a fake flowering tree separated her from them, providing a convenient cover as she listened in on their conversation.

"Did you *see* who Rob's dancing with?"

The remark came from Kerrie's friend, the woman Rachel still couldn't place.

"I couldn't care less." Kerrie's remark sounded like sour grapes. But it was her next comment that set Rachel on edge. "I've got my eyes on Todd Andrews."

Her friend let out an exclamation of surprise.

"I mean, have you ever seen a man that fabulous before? He looks like a Greek god or something."

Rachel cringed at the reference, but she would be the last to deny Todd's considerable magnetism.

"Well, Kerrie, I hate to tell you, but Todd's eyes are on—"

"I'm not worried about Rachel Anders," Kerrie snapped, cutting off her friend. "*She's* no competition."

Rachel's cheeks felt on fire from the sudden anger that rose in her breast. She barely heard Kerrie's last crude remark before the two friends drifted off.

"How about a dance, Rachel?"

Rachel whirled around to discover a tall, thin man standing beside her. "Sidney," she said, her anger melting into disappointment.

Sidney Wetherly. In high school, he'd been the kid who always stayed in the shadow of others. Like Mickey. No, not exactly like Mickey. While Mickey at least had a few friends, Sidney appeared to have none.

Yet there was one thing that distinguished Sidney in Rachel's mind. Through much of high school, he'd relentlessly pursued her. Never mind that she was Jeff's steady. Never mind that she'd never offered Sidney the slightest encouragement. His persistence might have been touching, might have garnered a certain sympathy on her part, except that he'd acted so irritatingly smug.

He had seemed convinced that she would one day see things his way. He'd sent her cards at every holiday and on no occasion in particular. Their senior year he had sent her flowers and candy in an apparent all-out bid for her attention.

Then, after graduation, he had disappeared from her life. In time she'd forgotten about him. And she'd been so worried about what she'd do if she saw Jeff at the reunion, she hadn't even given Sidney a thought. Not until now.

He studied her from under a mop of straight, shaggy hair. His sports coat hung on him. Rachel recalled that his clothes had never fit him well, though he came from a wealthy family and could undoubtedly afford designer blazers and slacks. "Well, what do you say, Rachel?" he said impatiently. His hand came up as if he might touch her.

She took a step backward. "I . . . I'm sorry, Sidney. I'm waiting for someone."

He scowled. "Sure you are." His voice was accusing. "I saw you with Todd Andrews. Not Jeff." Sidney's lips pursed in a hard line. "But you'll get tired of Todd too. Then you'll remember me.'' Abruptly, before she could form an answer, he turned on his heel and strode off.

Rachel looked after him, dumbfounded. A hand on her shoulder drew her attention away from Sidney. It was Todd. He'd come back to her alone.

"What's the matter?" He regarded her closely.

She quickly shook her head. "Nothing." A terrible understatement, but how could she tell him about her encounter with Sidney, let alone Kerrie Bowles' declaration that he looked like a Greek god?

"Did you see Jeff again?" Todd persisted.

She shook her head. "No." That was the truth—for now. "I'm just surprised that Sue isn't with you."

Todd's face relaxed into a smile. Reaching for her hand, he said, "Don't worry. I left her in good company." He motioned toward the far side of the room.

Rachel saw Sue then. She was with Diane and Mickey again. Rachel wanted to ask Todd how his dance with Sue went, but she didn't. "Rob Ransom asked Mickey to dance."

"I saw. Mickey's changed so much. She looks great."

Rachel glanced at Todd. "Yes, she does." Was it possible Todd might like to ask Mickey for a dance too? But his gaze, and his fingers laced securely with hers, told her differently.

"You know, I shouldn't take up all of your time tonight, Rachel. But ever since I knew I'd be moving back to St. Paul, you've been on my mind." He appeared thoughtful. "I wanted to see you, even if I believed you'd be married to Jeff."

"I'd say my time is being put to very good use," she replied softly. At that moment, the band launched into another number. It was a familiar song, slow and dreamy, though one Rachel hadn't heard in a long time.

"It sounds like they're playing all the old favorites tonight, doesn't it?"

"Yes," she agreed, meeting Todd's eyes. She wondered if he was thinking of Stacey. But when he took her in his arms without asking, his attention seemed focused solely on her. As they began to dance, both his hands came to rest lightly at her waist and she reached up to loop her arms around his neck.

The hypnotic melody, the romantic words of the song, and Todd's nearness conspired to again set Rachel more than a bit off-balance. But her eyes still searched the corners of the ballroom. Who did she expect to see? Sue? Jeff? Sidney?

"I've always liked that song."

Todd's whispered words drew Rachel's thoughts back to him. "Mmm. Me too," she whispered back. Her eyes fluttered shut for an instant.

She wasn't even trying when she spied Jeff again. He stood on the opposite side of the room from where he'd been before. But his eyes were on her, only her.

She watched with a certain trepidation as his gaze followed her. Suddenly Todd led her in the other direction. Had it been on purpose? No matter; she said a silent prayer of gratitude.

Todd's mouth brushed against her hair and Rachel came a fraction more unglued. What a strange evening it had been—stranger than she would ever have anticipated. She wasn't sure which was more disturbing: Jeff's gaze on her in that old, arrogant way; her worry over Sue's feelings for Todd; or Kerrie Bowles' brash notions about him. Then there was Sidney and his odd fixation on her that a decade obviously hadn't altered.

Rachel nearly jumped when someone tapped her on the shoulder and said, "May I cut in?"

Before she turned her head, she knew it was Kerrie. That seductive voice was unmistakable. When she did look, Rachel saw that Kerrie was staring straight at Todd, her generous mouth wearing a sultry smile.

If only she could come up with a clever reply, Rachel thought with chagrin. Before she had the chance, Todd spoke.

"Maybe some other time, Kerrie."

Rachel wasn't sure she'd heard right, but his coolly polite answer must have left no room for doubt in Kerrie's mind. The smile fled, replaced by a pouty frown. Todd's hand came up to rest lightly at Rachel's neck. There was an unmistakable hint of possessiveness in the gesture and Rachel felt a certain sense of triumph. Kerrie looked daggers at her, then marched away.

Moving Rachel away a fraction from himself, Todd lowered his forehead to hers. "Would you like to go someplace? A place where we could talk without interruptions?"

"I'd love that." The words came out in a breathless rush.

Before the song ended, Todd guided her around the other dancing couples until they came to an open spot.

"I need to find my friends, Todd." Already Rachel dreaded facing Sue, telling her that she and Todd would be leaving the reunion. Even if they weren't as close as they used to be, she valued Sue's friendship. Soon she must have a talk with her.

"There they are." Todd gestured toward the table the four friends had occupied earlier.

When they approached, Diane got up. Mickey stayed seated.

"Well, look who's here!" Diane exclaimed. "Have you guys been having a good time or what?" She gave Rachel's hand a squeeze.

"We're having a good time," Rachel confirmed. "Where's Sue?"

"Dancing." The answer was Mickey's. She crossed her arms, her gaze traveling from Rachel to Todd.

Rachel sensed that Mickey was upset for some reason. Maybe Sue had said something to her. "I saw you dancing, Mickey, with Rob." Rachel bent to hug her friend, but Mickey didn't return the embrace.

"He wanted another," Diane revealed.

Before Rachel could respond to the news, Mickey declared, "Rob Ransom is a bore."

Rachel wondered again at Mickey's reaction. Mickey seemed adamant in her dislike of the man, but the look on her face hinted at some inner conflict of emotions. It suddenly struck Rachel that Mickey and Rob would make a strikingly attractive couple, though she was dubious about their compatibility.

"Well, I guess we'll be leaving," Rachel said at last, other topics obviously exhausted.

"Sure, go ahead," Diane urged with a smile.

"Could you tell Sue that I'll call her?" Rachel glanced toward the dance floor. She didn't find Sue in the crowd.

"Of course," Diane assured her. "Now promise me something, Rachel."

"Anything."

"Derek and I are planning a trip back to St. Paul in about a month. Can we all get together? I mean, just us girls?" Diane threw a grin Todd's way.

"That sounds great," Rachel said quickly. "What about you, Mickey?"

"Sure. Our addresses and phone numbers'll be in the souvenir book, right?"

"Mine is," Diane said.

"Mine too," Rachel added. "And Sue's should be. If not, I know where she lives."

"It's all set then," Diane confirmed.

After hugging Diane, Rachel turned to Todd. "Okay, I'm ready."

He shook both Diane's hand and Mickey's, then he led Rachel to an exit not far from the tables.

On their way through the lobby, Rachel and Todd stopped to pick up their souvenir books. "This should make for interesting reading," Todd said, thumbing quickly through the book's pages.

"On some dark and lonely night?" Rachel teased.

They were both laughing as they went out the huge revolving doors of the Quincy Inn.

Chapter Three

A cool breeze off the Mississippi fanned their faces while they waited for the valet to bring their cars around. Then, by agreement, Todd followed Rachel to her apartment building where she pulled into her parking space in the underground garage.

"Very nice," she commented as she slipped into the front passenger seat of Todd's sports car. The leather upholstery felt smooth to the touch and the snazzy appointments made her own six-year-old Corolla sedan look shabby by comparison.

"Thanks." Todd glanced at her. "It was a stretch for me, but I have a love affair with Preludes."

"You must be doing pretty well," she remarked, watching his profile as he merged with the traffic on the boulevard that ran by her building.

"I'm doing all right," he acknowledged. His head turned briefly toward her building. "Where do you live in there?"

"Apartment 809."

"I see you're moving up in the world," he rejoined. His hands held the steering wheel lightly.

"How about you, Todd? Are you moving up too?"

He laughed. "Way up. I just leased a twentieth-floor condo on Riverview."

They were almost neighbors, Rachel realized. Riverview Drive was three blocks east of her building. She thought back to the neighborhood where they had both grown up, a middle-class suburb of tree-lined streets and modest two-story homes. It had been a place where kids could play outside even after dark, where there had been almost no cause for concern over crime.

As if he'd read her mind, Todd asked, "Do you get back to Fair Oaks often?"

"Not very often. Only to visit a few neighbors. You knew Mom and Dad moved to San Francisco, didn't you?"

"I'd heard."

"The old neighborhood's changed, Todd."

"I know. The house next to Dad and Mom's was broken into last week. When I was a kid, we hardly ever locked our doors," he added softly.

"Your parents still live in the same house, don't they?"

He nodded. "I don't think they'll ever leave it. Did you know Rebecca lives in Detroit?"

"I'd heard. She graduated from Michigan State last year, didn't she?"

"Yes, and got married a week later."

Rachel detected dismay in Todd's answer. Maybe he didn't care for his sister's new husband, or maybe he feared her marriage would end as his had.

Todd eased the Prelude to a stop at a red light. He looked at Rachel, his features illumined by the neon glow of a restaurant sign. Was it her imagination or did his eyes reflect sadness? "Where's Mitchell now?" he asked.

Mitchell. Though she'd had a good relationship with her parents, she and her brother had never been close. It might have been because he was seven years older than she.

"In the Air Force. He's a career officer. It's about the only thing he ever wanted to do."

"So, he's achieved his goal." Todd's remark was casual, but his fingers tightened on the steering wheel as the light changed to green.

"Yes. He's in San Francisco with Mom and Dad at the moment, but he's been all over the world."

"Paris? London? Tokyo?" Todd smiled at her and she smiled back. "You know what, Rachel?"

"What?" she asked quietly.

"I like it here, in St. Paul." He paused. "There's a saying, isn't there? You can't go home again. I'm hoping it's not true."

Rachel sensed there were deeper feelings behind the lightly spoken words. "I think coming back can be a fresh start, Todd."

"A new job, a new condo, and . . . old friends." He gave her a long, sideways glance. His hand reached for hers and clasped it for a moment before letting go.

She loved the warmth of his touch. At the same time, she felt uneasy with the different way she saw him tonight. Not just as an old friend and classmate, but as something more. A man she'd been instantly attracted to, one she might even fall in love with.

"Where would you like to go?" His voice sounded a bit strained.

"I don't care." There was huskiness in her voice too.

"I suppose we could just cruise."

Rachel had to smile at that. "Like the gang used to do way back when."

The exchange seemed to break the tension between them and they both exclaimed at once, "The West Bank!"

Laughing, Todd said, "There's another saying, Rachel. Great minds think alike."

She knew what he meant. They both were remembering the trendy area near the university where Neillson High students hung out on weekends, pretending to be part of the more sophisticated college crowd.

"B. J.'s or Jasper's?" Todd asked, naming two of the popular cafés on the Minneapolis side of the river.

"Jasper's." Rachel thought of the small, intimate café where the wooden, high-backed booths bore the carved initials of generations of young lovers. Hers and Jeff's were there; no doubt Todd's and Stacey's were too.

"Do they still serve the best bratwurst sandwiches in town, Rachel?"

"I hope so. I haven't been to Jasper's lately," she confessed.

"We'll soon find out." Todd made a right turn at the next intersection and drove across the Washington Avenue Bridge that spanned the river. "I've always loved that view." He indicated the glitter of lights reflected in the water below.

"Me too." At the moment, the sight struck Rachel as absurdly romantic.

Within minutes, Todd swung the Prelude into the parking lot of Jasper's. He took the last available space.

The spicy aroma of sausages cooking on the grill greeted their noses as they entered the café. The place was comfortably full, but there was no waiting line—a good sign, Rachel thought, remembering the hour-long waits of some weekends in the past.

A hostess led them toward the back of the restaurant. As they walked by a table occupied by several girls in

Neillson High jackets, Rachel saw how the teenagers' eyes followed Todd covetously.

He seemed not to be aware of his magnetism, but Rachel could remember a time when she and her girl-friends had done the same thing, eyeing the good-looking university men. The girls probably mistook Todd for a U. of M. student. It made Rachel smile.

But her smile fled when the hostess indicated for them to be seated at a booth in a back corner. It was right next to the one where she and Jeff had carved their initials. Rachel averted her gaze for a moment.

''What's wrong?'' Todd looked at her intently.

How many times had she caused him to ask that question tonight? *He must think I'm nuts.* She forced herself to smile as brightly as she could. ''Nothing. It just seems like old times being here.''

His face relaxed into a smile. ''It does,'' he agreed. Then his expression changed. ''I'm ready to make some new memories. How about you?''

A lump filled Rachel's throat, making it impossible for her to reply.

The waitress appeared just then, dressed in the Jasper's uniform of striped referee's shirt and black pants. She plopped two menus down on the table, winking at Todd as she told him she'd give them a couple of minutes.

Rachel opened her menu and made a pretense of studying it. ''What are you having?'' she asked at last, daring a glance at Todd.

He was gazing at her instead of the menu. ''The brat-wurst, of course. You?''

''I'll have the same.''

He took the menu from her hands and laid it on the table along with his. The waitress reappeared to write their orders, then came back a second time with iced mugs of root beer.

Todd took a draft of the root beer from his mug. Curling his fingers around the frosted glass, he said, "Tell me about Cabbage Rose's. Tell me about you, Rachel. What made you decide you wanted your own business?"

"You thought I'd be an accountant, like Dad."

"Guilty as charged." He grinned at her.

"I assure you that my accounting courses didn't go to waste. I always had the dream of opening a small clothing boutique. Another dream I've had is to learn fashion design. I never fulfilled that dream." She ran a finger around the rim of her mug.

"Maybe not, but you've done the next best thing. Right?"

Rachel nodded in agreement. At times, it was hard for her to believe that she owned her own business. Todd's reassurance was good to hear. "The clothes I sell aren't new. Cabbage Rose's is a consignment boutique," she explained.

"Where's your shop located?"

"In the Penny Lane Arcade."

Todd gave her a sharp look. Should she interpret it as admiration? "In old town, as we used to say," he remarked.

Their sandwiches came and they were occupied briefly with choosing condiments from a tray the waitress placed in front of them.

Todd lifted his sandwich, dripping mustard and relish, to his mouth and took a bite. Rachel did the same.

"Mmm. It's better than I remembered."

"It is," she concurred, looking over at him. There was a streak of yellow on his nice firm jaw. She tried to stifle a giggle, all the while thinking of Kerrie Bowles' comment. If she could, she'd inform Kerrie that Todd Andrews wasn't a Greek god after all, just a very handsome man who wore a dash of mustard well.

"Okay, what is it this time?" Todd's eyes sparkled with amusement.

"Nothing." She waved her hands. "Just mustard." Impulsively, she picked up her napkin and reached over to dab the offending streak from his chin.

"If you're going to do that, I hope my whole face gets plastered with relish."

His quip brought an appropriate response. She blushed.

That made him grin even more broadly. "Now as you were saying, your shop is in Penny Lane." He set his sandwich down and leaned back against the booth, folding his arms in a familiar way.

How many times had she seen him sit just like that in homeroom or economics class?

"How are the rents in that area, Rachel? That is, if you don't mind my asking."

"Reasonable enough. I've built up something of a clientele there too." With someone she didn't know, she might interpret his questions as nosiness. But Todd was a developer. He would naturally be interested in such details. Maybe she should introduce him to Meg.

"My grandparents left an inheritance," she went on. "Mom and Dad loaned me a healthy part of their share to open Cabbage Rose's. You can't know how appreciative I am of that. Or how scared it makes me sometimes," she added, looking away.

"You want your shop to be successful," Todd offered quietly. His hand touched her arm, bringing her attention back to him. His eyes captured hers. "I know how you feel. Mom went back to work as a secretary to help put me through Cal State."

"You had a scholarship." Rachel recalled his excitement on learning he'd received the City League award. He'd even hugged her—and she'd thought nothing of it.

"It helped," he acknowledged, "but the money paid

only part of my tuition. I worked through college, washing dishes in the campus cafeteria.''

She had to laugh at the image that conjured up. "I'll bet you looked great in an apron, Todd.''

"Like a model for Soup Kitchens International," he shot back. "Hey, we'd better eat our sandwiches before they get cold.''

"Ugh. Cold, greasy bratwurst." She gave a mock shudder and Todd chuckled.

They fell silent, polishing off their sandwiches. When the last bite was down, Rachel pushed her plate aside. Todd stacked his on top of hers. "Force of habit." He looked at her expectantly.

Rachel decided it was her turn to ask questions. "Just what is it you'll be developing in our fair city?" The steady blue of Todd's gaze almost made her blush again. She regretted the way she'd worded the question. "Or should I rephrase that?''

He laughed, but his answer was serious. "Have you heard about the proposed Kilborn Atrium?''

That drew a surprised reaction from her. "I've heard a lot about it. Mostly controversial.''

Todd's mouth drooped a little. "I was afraid of that. Silverthorne has gotten the proverbial black eye lately, but it's not deserved.''

"I don't have much of an opinion on it, Todd," she answered honestly, lest he think she was prejudiced. "But I understand the project will take down a number of houses in the historical district. I hate to see that happen." She toyed with her napkin, finally folding it and setting her mug on it.

"Silverthorne is willing to pay the expense of relocating every one of those homes. Eight or ten at the most is all that would be affected." He clasps his hands together, earnestness evident in his expression.

Rachel didn't doubt that he was convinced of the sincerity of Silverthorne's promise. She wished she could be.

When she made no reply, Todd went on, "The new park on Riverside would be the perfect spot for those houses. The park borders a portion of the already existing historical district."

"You sound like a politician."

He made a face. "I don't mean to."

"I know," she was quick to assure him. His hair tumbled down in front a little, covering part of his forehead. It made him look very young. "I hope you're right, Todd. I wouldn't want to think that—"

The waitress interrupted Rachel. "Sorry, guys. We close in five minutes." She smiled sympathetically.

Rachel checked her watch. "It's nearly one," she said, stunned at how late it was.

"So it is," Todd agreed, glancing at his own watch. He stretched, obviously reluctant to get up. "Are you tired, Rachel?"

She hadn't even thought about it. "No, not at all."

"Good. I'm not ready for this night to end. What do you say?"

"I'm not either." She felt a tingle of excitement. He didn't want to leave her yet. "Where can we go? We're about to be kicked out of here." She regarded the waitress who was tapping her toe on the linoleum floor.

"What's open? I'd suggest Como Park, but . . . "

"We might get mugged," Rachel finished for him. She had a sudden idea. "Henley Plaza! Have you heard about the Plaza or seen it yet?"

"Yes and no."

"It's fabulous, Todd. Open twenty-four hours a day and they've got a huge roof garden that's thirty stories up."

"Show me the way." He grabbed her hand as he slid out of the booth.

The drive to the plaza took no more than fifteen minutes. Traffic was light and there was ample parking in the well-lit garage.

With Rachel leading the way, they went straight to the elevator in the richly appointed mezzanine. The floor was deserted except for a few other couples strolling about and several security guards.

"Glass," Todd said appreciatively, running his hand along the side of the elevator door.

"Watch." Rachel punched the button for the thirtieth floor. The elevator soared skyward, offering a breathtaking, if rapid, view of flower-filled balconies, shining storefronts, and copper statues as it passed the various stories.

The door opened and they stepped out amid a lush display of orchids and other tropical plants. The air was sweetly scented, but more chilly, the wind sharper at this level hundreds of feet above the sidewalk.

"This reminds me of Nasby Commons in Seattle," Todd said, reaching out to touch a purple bloom.

Rachel was aware that his other arm had come around her waist. "Then Nasby Commons must be beautiful."

"Not as beautiful as up here."

They began to stroll along a cobblestone path. Flowering trees and shrubs hugged either side of the walkway. In the distance was the faint sound of bubbling water.

"Over here," Rachel urged, tugging on Todd's arm. He followed her to a three-tiered fountain. Tiny waterfalls fell over the scalloped, pastel edges of what looked like giant seashells. In the middle of the fountain, water gushed from a towering marble cone.

From the fountain the lights of the Twin Cities were visible, spread out below like jewels on a dark carpet.

Rachel shivered, prompting a soft, "You're cold," from Todd.

How could she explain that she really wasn't, that it was the spectacular sight, the fact she was sharing it with him, that sent a chill through her? She chose to say nothing, instead leaning against him as he took off his coat and draped it around her shoulders.

His arm held her securely. "This is fantastic, Rachel," he whispered.

She wasn't sure if he meant the roof garden, the cities sprawled below—or whether he too felt something not easily put into words.

"The Plaza was finished just over two years ago. The first time I came here, I was with Jeff." Why had she said that? Rachel wished she could snatch back the words.

Todd swiftly pulled her around to face him. "What happened between you and Jeff?" he asked almost brusquely.

Tiny wrinkles knitted his brow. He knows what it feels like, Rachel told herself. She cleared her throat. "It's hard to explain. I . . . Jeff changed.

"How?" Todd pressed gently. His hands rested now on her arms under the fabric of the coat. "I remember Jeff as intense. The 'doctor.' "

"He's that, all right." She gave a short, ironic laugh. "But this was different. I noticed it right after we started at the U. of M. Jeff became possessive of me. Not just the usual kind of stuff," she hastened to add. "You know, the petty jealousy a lot of couples experience."

"I understand. You don't have to explain." Todd's thumbs made slow circles on her wrists.

Another shiver started at the tip of Rachel's spine as she suddenly remembered the way Jeff had watched her while she and Todd danced. "He would always question me about things like where I'd been if I was out when he called. At first, he acted like he was only joking, but later it was no joke.'' She bit her lip. "He became demanding, even verbally abusive.''

"Why should he have been suspicious of *you?*'' There was anger—and disbelief—in Todd's voice.

"I never gave him any reason to be. He just was. As time passed, it got worse. We'd become engaged the beginning of our junior year, though we hadn't planned to marry for a couple of more years. We agreed we wanted to pay back at least some of our student loans first.''

"Go on,'' Todd urged softly.

"Well, knowing that I wasn't rushing into marriage gave me a chance to stand back and see what was happening between Jeff and me. I didn't like what I saw.'' She sighed. Todd's response was to draw her closer, sheltering her as if he wanted to protect her from the pain of remembering the past.

Rachel closed her eyes for a moment. Finally, she said, "I had to recognize that I couldn't live with a man who suspected my every move.''

"No one should live with someone like that.'' Todd's declaration brooked no argument.

A thought occurred to Rachel. Was Stacey like that too?

Todd let out a long breath. "It's a funny thing, Rachel, about Stacey and me. Did you know we got married while I was at Cal State?'' Rachel shook her head. "We were both far too young to appreciate what sacrifices have to be made in a marriage, what it means to truly put your mate's happiness ahead of your own.'' He grew silent. "I tried, Rachel. But maybe it was too late.''

"I believe you.'' Her response held a determined loyalty that she might have questioned another time. Yet she was certain Todd was being truthful.

"Stacey took a two-year program and got an associate degree in business administration,'' he continued. "I didn't blame her for that. I'm excited about my career too. But she seemed not to care anymore about building a life together. Then she met a guy where she worked. I guess he gave her something I couldn't.''

Rachel couldn't imagine what that might be. ''I'm sorry,'' she whispered. Todd had lowered his eyes to a study of the lights below, but she doubted he really saw them.

''I wanted a family, Rachel, the fun of doing things together, like walks in the park or visiting the zoo.''

It sounded wonderful to her. ''I'm sure you'll have that one day, Todd.''

His eyes came back to hers. ''What I said earlier about making new memories. . . . ''

A sudden gust of wind tore past them, unusually strong and cold for late June. It shook the leaves on the trees and sent water from the fountain spraying against them.

Todd appeared distracted by the sudden change in the weather. ''What happens when winter comes, Rachel?'' He cradled her near. ''Do all the trees and flowers up here just die?''

She suspected that wasn't the question he wanted to ask. ''They put a bubble over the roof. For these trees and flowers, it's eternal summer.''

She must have given him the right answer. Without another word, he lowered his mouth to hers.

As he held her tight, her arms came up to circle his neck. Through their clothing she could feel his heart beating against hers, and she was sure she had never been kissed in quite the same way before.

Chapter Four

"Who is he, Rach?"

Rachel stopped in the middle of taking down one of Lucy Benson's dresses. "Who is *who?*" she asked, smiling a little, her head turned away from Meg.

"The guy who put that glow in your eyes. You *are* glowing, Rachel." Meg touched her friend's arm. "Someone you met at the reunion, true? Let's see," she went on, not waiting for an answer, "the guy you'd barely noticed in high school, that shy, skinny kid everyone thought was a loser, then—" Meg snapped her fingers. "He metamorphosed into man of the year and when you saw him, it was love at first gasp."

Rachel laughed, shaking her head. "No, Meg, not him."

Meg's eyes widened. "You mean there was a guy like that in your class?"

"Uh-huh. His name's Rob Ransom."

"Hmm. Rob Ransom. He sounds interesting. But if

45

not him, then who?'' Meg threw her arms in the air, her real reason for stopping at the boutique seemingly forgotten.

"Here, you go change.'' Rachel gave her friend a gentle push toward a curtained-off booth in the back of the shop. "I'll hand you things to try on.''

"And tell me about *him* at the same time.''

"Agreed.'' Rachel selected a purple silk pantsuit. "Try this on first.'' She shoved the suit around the side of the curtain and felt Meg grab it. "His name is Todd Andrews.''

"Andrews. That's a lot like Anders.''

"I know. He sat behind me in most of our classes from first grade through senior year. I remember him as a tease. He did stuff like planting dead spiders in my desk and getting my hair in the finger paint.''

"Todd sounds like a charmer.'' Meg poked her head around the curtain, grinning. "And I'll bet he had a terrible crush on you before he was old enough to tell time.''

"That's kind of what Mickey said, though I doubt it.''

Meg shot her a puzzled glance. "Mickey?''

"Oh, she was one of my girlfriends in high school. I'll tell you about her some other day. It's quite a story too.'' Rachel smiled. "Actually, Todd started going with someone, a girl named Stacey, right after Jeff and I got involved. Later, he and Stacey got married.''

"Married?'' Meg's eyes registered surprise.

"He's not married now. Todd's divorced. She left him.''

"Oh.'' Meg looked relieved. "You scared me for a minute.''

Rachel pushed Meg back into the booth with a mild shove. "Get the suit on and I'll tell you more.'' She paused until she heard Meg doing up the long zipper on the suit. "Todd came over to me at the reunion. It was pretty much unexpected. In fact, another of my friends, Sue—you've heard me talk about her . . . '' She waited for Meg's ''yes,'' then continued. ''Sue was the one who'd always cared for Todd. But when he asked me to dance, I couldn't refuse.''

''Of course you couldn't,'' Meg retorted from inside the booth.

''We danced . . . and *danced*.'' Rachel almost lost herself for a moment in the memory of how natural it had felt to be in Todd's arms. It had seemed as if it was where she belonged. More guilt feelings rose at the idea. Shouldn't Sue be having the happy memory instead of her?

''Then what?'' Meg coaxed impatiently as she stepped around the curtain.

The sight of Meg in the suit stunned Rachel, causing her to forget her train of thought for a second. ''You look super!''

''You think?'' Meg eyed herself critically in a large standing mirror.

''It was made for you.''

''No, it was made for Lucy Benson,'' Meg shot back, causing Rachel to giggle. ''But you've convinced me. I'll take it. What else have you got?'' Meg held up her hand when Rachel started to turn away. ''Only after you've told me what happened next with Todd.''

Rachel leaned against the wall with a sigh. ''We left the reunion early and went to the West Bank, to Jasper's where a lot of us used to hang out.''

''Sounds promising so far.''

''We talked and ate bratwurst sandwiches.''

''And after Jasper's?''

Rachel closed her eyes briefly. The remembrance of what happened next was a little too vivid. ''We drove to Henley Plaza and went up to the roof garden.''

"Wow!" Meg enthused. "Is that a romantic spot or what?"

"It's a romantic spot," Rachel agreed, hurrying to fetch a red belted dress with a softly flared skirt. "Here, try this one next." Maybe the dress would serve as a distraction for Meg.

It didn't, though Meg took the dress and disappeared into the booth again. "Did the roof garden have the desired effect on Todd?"

Rachel wasn't about to ask Meg what she meant by "desired effect"; she knew her friend well enough to imagine. "He'd never been there before," she hedged. "But I'm sure he was duly impressed."

Meg stuck her head out from the curtain. "You're cagy, you know that, don't you?" She flashed Rachel a grin.

Just then Rachel heard the door of the boutique open. When she turned to see who was there, she couldn't believe her eyes. "Todd!" she blurted without thinking.

He came toward her, clad in a dark-blue polo shirt and jeans that did nothing to hide his long, muscular legs.

Rachel watched, entranced. Only later did she scold herself for taking an undue interest in Todd's build. Remembering Meg, she tore her eyes from Todd and looked back. Her friend was staring too, but Meg's head disappeared back into the booth just before Todd stopped in front of it.

"I hope you don't mind that I dropped in on you."

"No," Rachel managed to say, aware that her hands trembled slightly. "I don't mind." *That* was an understatement.

"Remember I promised that I'd see you soon?" He gave her a smile while his eyes gazed at her appreciatively.

"I remember." How could she forget when he'd made

the promise right after he'd kissed her good-bye at her door? If he'd asked, she could have told him the exact minute. It had been four-fifteen A.M., Sunday morning. She'd checked her watch just as they'd emerged from the elevator onto her floor.

But she couldn't believe that he was keeping his promise so soon. She'd even wondered if he might have been caught up in the nostalgia of the evening they'd unexpectedly shared and had no real intention of contacting her again.

Todd's smile faded a bit. "I can come back if you're busy." He glanced toward the booth.

"I'm not busy, just helping a friend," she said quickly, hoping he wouldn't leave. "Meg! Can you come out? I'd like you to meet someone."

Instantly, the curtain was pushed aside and Meg stepped from the booth wearing the red dress. Her attention immediately went to Todd.

"Todd, this is my best friend, Meg Simms. Meg, this is Todd Andrews."

Todd extended his hand; Meg took it. "Nice to meet you, Meg."

"You too." Meg smiled. "Rachel was just telling me about the reunion, and the fact that you were once fond of scaring innocent little girls with nasty spiders."

Rachel grimaced; Todd shot her a curious look. "Sometimes I call her Meggy Blunt," she said weakly.

That drew a chuckle from Todd. "What do you call *me* now, Rachel?"

She wasn't prepared for his quietly worded question. Warmth flooded her cheeks under the blue of his gaze. She didn't dare say what first came to her mind. "Meg's in real estate too," she said in a hasty attempt to derail her runaway emotions.

The revelation must have aroused Todd's interest. He

turned to Meg, giving Rachel a chance to compose herself. "What company, Meg?"

"Plymouth. And you?" Meg looked equally interested.

"Silverthorne."

The word seemed to drop in the sudden silence that filled the room. Rachel sensed a subtle change in Meg's demeanor, perhaps not enough for Todd to notice. But definitely there. Was it because of the recent controversy over the Kilborn project?

"I'd better be going, Rachel."

Todd's abrupt announcement took Rachel by surprise. Maybe he'd detected Meg's diffidence, after all. At the same time, her heart sank; she almost reached out to hold him there.

"No, I have to go," Meg put in. "I've got a house to show in half an hour."

Rachel stared at Meg. Strange that her friend hadn't mentioned she was on a tight schedule until this moment. Had she made up the appointment as an excuse to leave?

Meg went on, "I'll take this dress and the suit today, and I'll be back tomorrow to try on the rest of the stuff." She paused before heading into the booth again. "I'll see you around, Todd." The words were coolly polite.

Rachel was growing more anxious. There were crosscurrents at work between Meg and Todd that she didn't understand.

She and Todd had been classmates; they'd just shared one fantastic evening together—nothing more. Why should she be so upset because Meg hadn't been bowled over by him? Maybe harder to answer was why Todd stood stolidly in place, his eyes telling her that he'd welcome Meg's hasty departure.

When Meg left the booth, dress clutched in her hand, Rachel led her to the register and rung up the sale. Then

Meg said a quick farewell and, without so much as a glance back at Todd, left the shop.

While trying to compose herself, Rachel made a pretense of smoothing a wrinkle on a dress that hung on a display hook. From behind her, she heard Todd clear his throat.

"What do you think of Cabbage Rose's?" she asked finally, facing him.

"I'm impressed." Todd leaned against the counter, his chin cupped in one hand. He wore an expression of bemusement. "I assume Cabbage Rose is the lady sitting in the window."

Rachel regarded the doll fondly. "She belonged to my great-grandmother."

"I'd say that Cabbage Rose is a most fitting symbol for your boutique."

"I'm glad you like her." Rachel's attention was drawn back to Todd when he touched her arm.

"Yes. I like Cabbage Rose . . . and you." He paused. "But I don't think your friend, Meg, likes me very much."

Rachel had no desire to pursue the idea, not until she had a chance to talk to Meg alone. "Should I call you Todd Blunt?" she said, hoping to deflect any concern he might have.

"I really don't care what you call me," he said with ease. "I amend that. I *do* care. You know, I love to listen to you talk."

She suddenly felt warm again. Why did he have to affect her this way? "I don't believe anyone's ever paid me that particular compliment before." She raised her eyes to meet his. "But then, I've been doing an awful lot of talking around you, haven't I?"

His hand came up to claim hers. "I'd like for you to do a lot more, Rachel. And I meant it when I said I wanted to see your store. You've done a great job."

"Thank you." She couldn't say which pleased her most: his words or the feel of his fingers enclosing hers.

"Another reason I came is because I was wondering if you'd go to dinner with me Friday. That is, if you don't have plans." A flicker of uncertainty marred the sky blue of his eyes.

"I'd love to have dinner with you." The fast reply must have told him she hadn't needed to debate the matter. His smile returned. Rachel remembered something he'd said at Henley Plaza. "Have you been to the zoo since you've returned home?"

"No. Is this an invitation?"

"I guess it is."

"How can I refuse when your last one had such an invigorating effect on me?"

His remark made her blush deepen, much to her chagrin. She knew very well he meant their visit to the roof garden. "This excursion might have a chilling effect instead."

Todd looked intrigued. "In what way?"

"They've just expanded the Antarctic exhibit. A passel of penguins, stupendous icebergs, even a walk-through model of McMurdo Station. I recommend we take our winter coats."

"I'll bring mine. You won't need yours."

It was impossible for her to think of an answer to that. They both started laughing. The thought entered her mind that she and Jeff had never enjoyed such easy bantering back and forth in all the years they'd dated.

Todd glanced at his watch. "I have to go." He sounded regretful. "I've got to run an errand, then it's back to work for the evening." Gazing down at her, he said, "Could you close early on Friday? I'll be off at noon."

"Yes, I could close early Friday." At the moment, if

he'd asked her to close for the whole week, she'd be tempted to oblige.

"Good." He squeezed her hand. "Do you want me to pick you up here or at your apartment?"

"Why don't you come by the apartment, say about one?"

"Perfect."

Rachel walked him to the door. Sounds of blaring horns, the hum of conversation, and laughter from the sidewalk filtered into the shop.

Todd took a step to leave, then turned back to her. Lowering his head, his lips touched hers for an instant. "See you on Friday," he said softly, and was gone.

The remembrance of his other kisses kept Rachel anchored to the spot, her eyes on him as he merged with the rush-hour traffic. "See you," she whispered, though he couldn't hear her. She watched until she could no longer distinguish his blond head from others in the crowd.

"Todd is a dangerously handsome man, Rach."

Rachel stopped in the middle of her task of rehanging a dress. "Dangerously?" She tossed the word in the direction of the changing booth. Even before Meg had come into the shop, Rachel had decided she wouldn't broach the subject of Todd Andrews. Now it seemed she didn't have a choice. "You make handsomeness sound like a disease, Meg."

Meg came out of the booth with a grin and an armload of dresses and suits. "I want all of these."

Rachel took the garments and headed for the counter at the back of the boutique. Meg followed. "Why dangerously?" she persisted as she laid the purchases beside the register.

Meg's expression grew uncustomarily serious. "Because with a glance, any woman could fall hard. Like you.''

Was it that obvious? ''How do you know I've fallen for Todd Andrews?''

Meg shot her an incredulous look. ''Come on, Rach. You never were good at keeping secrets. By the way, you two make a fantastic couple.''

''I'm not sure that's a compliment,'' Rachel replied carefully. ''Yesterday, when you met Todd, I got the impression you didn't care for him.''

Reaching out, Meg patted Rachel's hand. ''No, it's not Todd himself. It's the fact he's working for Silverthorne.''

Relief warred with anxiety in Rachel's mind. At least she knew her notions had been correct. ''I was afraid of that. I guess they don't have the best reputation in town, do they?''

''Best? They've probably got the worst.'' Meg's expression showed distaste. ''Let me clue you in on A. Bradley Silverthorne, Jr. He's a master at power games. And he doesn't play by the rules; he makes up his own.''

''But isn't that common with companies like Silverthorne?'' Rachel instantly regretted the question. ''I don't mean to imply that—''

''That everyone in the business is rubbing his palms together too.'' Meg smiled understandingly. ''I know what you mean, Rach. And yes, there are no doubt under-the-table deals going on in certain companies, especially when a plum contract is at stake. I suppose the temptation is always there.''

Meg spread her hands in front of her. She studied the impeccably polished nails. ''Silverthorne goes beyond what's considered borderline ethical,'' she said quietly. ''Bradley pushes the limits of the law. A good example is the Kilborn Atrium project.''

Rachel gripped Meg's arm. "That's the one Todd's been assigned to."

A look of dismay crossed Meg's face. "He told you that?"

"Yes. He said they hired him as the developer on the Atrium."

"He won't be the only developer on the project," Meg responded hastily. "No doubt he's under the supervision of someone with more experience."

That piece of information did nothing to soothe Rachel's mind. "I don't want Todd to get hurt, Meg. Professionally . . . or personally. I won't deny that I'm very attracted to him, but I've also known Todd a long time, way before I realized I had any feelings for him." And it had been far less complicated to think of him just as a classmate, a casual friend, she could have added.

"I'm not questioning Todd's honesty." Meg's eyes grew large with concern. "I'm sure Silverthorne did a good P.R. job when they interviewed him. There are several guys like Todd with Plymouth. They're talented, enthusiastic, eager to make a reputation for themselves. That's not bad. It's just . . . "

"It's just that Silverthorne has a tarnished reputation and some of the tarnish could rub off on Todd. Isn't that what you're trying to say?"

Meg took hold of Rachel's hand. "I'm afraid it *will,* Rach. I'd hate to see that happen. For Todd's sake. And yours," she added softly.

There seemed nothing more Rachel could say. Turning from her friend, she continued adding up the purchases. But her thoughts were on Meg's ominous prediction. Was Todd the kind of person who could so easily be swayed by power and money that he'd do something unethical?

"Rach, I hope you're not angry with me." Meg's voice sounded contrite.

Rachel stopped her tallying and met her friend's eyes. "Of course I'm not angry. We're friends and friends are frank with each other." She gave Meg a reassuring hug.

"It's only because I care about you so much that I told you about Silverthorne."

"I know." Rachel completed her calculations. In an attempt to lighten the somber mood between them, she said, "I'm afraid you owe me two hundred and seventy-two dollars and thirty-five cents."

Meg feigned horror. "Do you know this dalliance with Lucy Benson's wardrobe is going to wipe out my food budget for the next month? And it's the thirty-five cents that did it," she added with mock seriousness. "I'll have to subsist on beans and tap water for weeks. No Perrier."

Rachel laughed despite herself. "You're silly."

Meg winked and got out her checkbook. After the check and garments were exchanged, Rachel walked her friend to the front of the store.

Meg hesitated. "Maybe we could have lunch or dinner together next week sometime."

Rachel smiled. "Sounds great. But how will you pay?"

"I thought it would be your treat." Meg grinned. "Or I could bring my apron and wash dishes."

The innocent remark provoked an image in Rachel's mind. Her smile faded.

"What's wrong?" Meg looked anxious.

"Nothing. Just something Todd said about washing dishes."

"You do have it bad, don't you?" Meg sympathized.

Rachel took Meg by the shoulders and propelled her to the door. Opening it, she said, "Call me," in a way that implied the subject of Todd Andrews was closed.

Meg left with a wave, heading down the busy sidewalk. Rachel shut the door and collapsed against it. She felt drained, her temples drawn tight from the beginnings of a headache.

After a moment, she went to the stockroom and shook two aspirin from a bottle she kept there. Taking them with several swallows of water, Rachel tried to shut out of her mind the troubling things Meg had told her. For the first time in a long time, she'd begun to feel optimistic about the future, her personal future to be exact. Todd had come along from out of the past, seemingly ready to take her heart by storm. But would she soon regret the torrent of emotions he stirred in her?

She did already regret them in one way. If it wasn't enough to worry about Todd's involvement with Silverthorne, she had her conscience needling her about the matter of contacting Sue.

Hadn't she promised she would call her friend and set a time to get together? She must learn soon whether Sue still cared for Todd.

Once she had picked up the phone and started to dial Sue's number, then stopped. She'd argued back and forth with herself. Hadn't she tried to push Todd in Sue's direction at the reunion? And hadn't he come right back to her? The fact the answers were still "yes" and "yes" didn't diminish her guilt feelings nor her sense of alarm over Sue's bone thinness.

The aspirin finally took effect; her headache eased. Rachel vowed to herself that she would call Sue right after the weekend. For now she would try mightily to block the subject from her mind.

By Friday morning Rachel was feeling less guilty and more looking forward to her date with Todd, so much so that she decided not to go in to the boutique at all.

She slept in until nine, then got up and took a leisurely bath. Todd hadn't said where they would eat dinner, but since they were visiting the zoo first, Rachel guessed they'd wind up someplace that was informal. Secretly, she hoped for Pasta and candlelight at an intimate Italian café.

She debated for a couple of minutes before deciding on one of her better pairs of jeans and a red crew top. If Todd wanted to take her to a fancy restaurant, she could always change into something more formal after their visit to the zoo. After brushing her hair, she took a curling iron and curved the ends under. An appraising look in the mirror told Rachel the simple style suited her casual dress.

In the kitchen, she fixed herself a hearty brunch of pancakes, bacon, and fresh fruit. That would hold her until dinner.

It was hard not to keep tabs on the time while she ate and read the morning paper. The hands on her kitchen clock barely seemed to budge and Rachel found herself wishing it was one already. For a moment she imagined how Todd might look standing in the doorway, greeting her with that gorgeous smile. A telltale sigh escaped her lips.

The paper dutifully read and dirty dishes loaded into the dishwasher, she decided to go down to the lobby and check her mailbox even though the postman didn't usually come that early.

But to her surprise Rachel found her box was full of mail. She took the stack upstairs to her apartment and put it on her desk to sort. There didn't appear to be anything exciting, just the common assortment of bills and a few advertisements and sweepstakes promotions. One envelope was from Mineola Property Company, the group that managed Penny Lane. Opening it, she discovered a two-page tenants' survey inside. More busywork, Rachel thought with a grimace.

At the bottom of the pile was a plain envelope with only her name and address typed on the outside. There was no return address. Rachel turned it over in her hands. It didn't look like a bill. Maybe it was a teaser kind of ad telling her she'd just won a trip to the Caribbean.

Smiling at the thought, she tore open the envelope and shook out the contents. A neatly folded piece of paper fell onto the desk. Unfolding it, she saw the page was blank except for several lines typed in the middle.

As Rachel read them under her breath, her smile turned into a puzzled frown.

" *'When, in disgrace with fortune and men's eyes,*
I all alone beweep my outcast state. . . . ' "
     Pausing, she went on, " *'Do you remember*
those words, Rachel? You should. I'll be watching
you.' "

Rachel gazed at the lines, repeating them again in her mind. There was no name, no clue as to who had sent the strange message—or why. Shakespeare. The first lines were the famous poet's, weren't they? She'd never been big on poetry. *Do you remember those words, Rachel?* the note said. Should she?

Then suddenly it occurred to her who must have sent the note. Really, it was absurdly simple. Hadn't Todd confessed at the reunion that he'd been watching her all evening? And though he'd always been a tease, maybe the mysterious message wasn't meant so much as a joke as it was a reminder of the evening they'd shared.

Smiling again, Rachel refolded the paper and set it aside. Why Todd had quoted lines of poetry she couldn't say, but she would find out soon enough.

Todd came right on time, dressed very much as she'd imagined he would be, in jeans and a jade knit shirt. At the sight of him standing in her doorway, every nagging thought of Silverthorne and shady business dealings, any stray wisp of guilt over Sue, fled Rachel's mind like darkness before the sun.

Todd's hair looked burnished against the green of his shirt and his tan only enhanced the effect. "Come in," she invited, a bit breathless.

"I thought today would never get here," he said, not moving from where he stood.

"But it did." Rachel didn't say that she had thought this *moment* would never get here. "Would you like to sit down for a little while? I could get you coffee or a soda.

He stepped inside. "Thanks, but why don't we stop later at the Pavilion, after we've visited the penguins and icebergs."

"Okay." The Pavilion was the zoo's snack bar, a colorful tentlike building that served sandwiches, drinks, and popcorn.

Todd looked around the living room. "You've got a nice apartment."

The way he had his hands clasped together in front of him gave Rachel the idea he might be feeling a bit shy. "I like my apartment," she replied, taking the several steps to her desk. She reached behind her back to retrieve the cryptic note. If Todd was at all uneasy, what she was about to say should banish it. "I thought you might want to know that I received some interesting mail today."

"What kind of mail?" He turned his attention to her.

Rachel almost wavered under his inquisitive gaze. "A very intriguing message. Something you might be familiar with, Todd. I wonder who this could be from." Unable to resist, she handed him the note.

His look of curiosity turned into one of perplexity. "What do you mean?"

"A couple of lines from Shakespeare. A small confession." She was purposely baiting him. "Read it," she urged.

Todd's eyes dropped to a study of the piece of paper. After a moment, he looked back at her. "You think I wrote this?"

"I *know* it was you, though I admit the lines of poetry bewilder me. Are they from Shakespeare?"

Todd combed his fingers through his hair. "Oh, the words are the Bard's, all right." A wry smile crossed his lips. "Don't you remember, Rachel? Sophomore English, the Elizabethan festival?" He took a step closer to her.

Rachel had to tilt her head back to see his face. The question about the authorship of the note was momentarily forgotten. It was strange that she hadn't thought of the festival until he reminded her. "I guess I wasn't all that taken with Shakespeare, but now that you mention it, I vaguely recall the occasion."

"But not enough to remember that you recited those words on stage." Pausing, Todd said in a lowered voice, " 'When, in disgrace with fortune and men's eyes, I all alone beweep my outcast state.' "

He recited the lines well, no doubt better than she ever had. She was the one beginning to feel ill at ease. Laughing, she said, "I must have blocked my, uh, performance from my mind. But why do you remember it after so many years? Was I that bad?"

Todd's eyes took on a darker hue as his gaze roved over her face, settling on her lips. "Bad? You were wonderful, I'm sure. But it wasn't your acting skill that made me remember, Rachel. It was because at that moment, when you were onstage, I knew that I loved you."

Rachel's eyes widened; her lips parted in a gasp of surprise. "Knew that you *loved* me?"

Todd turned slightly away from her, averting his eyes. His voice was still soft when he said, "I was standing offstage at the time. I was thinking that the poem was all wrong for you." His eyes came back to meet hers.

"And I realized how miscast the roles of Romeo and Juliet were."

Romeo and Juliet? What had she missed back then? How had she managed to be so oblivious to his feelings for her? She would be ashamed to admit she didn't know what part he had played in the festival, but she did know that she was already dating Jeff by that time. The mention of Shakespeare's tragic lovers did stir one memory. "Rob Ransom was Romeo, wasn't he?"

"And Kerrie Bowles was Juliet." Todd's face came close to hers; for a moment it seemed that he would kiss her. "I imagined you as Juliet." He left unsaid who should have played Romeo. Abruptly, he gave his attention back to the note in his hands.

Rachel felt unnerved by his revelation. Though she longed for him to say more on the subject, she knew a greater concern intruded on his thoughts. "There wasn't a return address on the envelope," she said shakily.

Todd frowned. "I wonder who would do this." He tapped the piece of paper. "Or why."

Maybe it was the way he said it, but Rachel suddenly shivered, as if they were already in the zoo's Antarctic exhibit instead of her warm, cheery apartment. "It must be a joke . . . don't you think?"

"It might be." His brow knitted in concentration.

"Obviously somebody who was also in our English class, right?"

After a brief silence, Todd replied, "Not necessarily. The other English classes were invited to watch the show that night."

"That's true," she conceded, biting her lip. "And now with the reunion just last week, it seems somebody besides you must have remembered my recitation of the poem." She searched Todd's face for agreement.

"That would seem logical." He handed the piece of paper back to her. "Keep this, Rachel. Just in case."

The way he said it almost made her tremble again. "In case what? You're making me feel kind of scared."

"No." The word was hushed as he swept her into his arms and nestled her close. "Please don't be frightened."

Rachel pressed her face against his shirt. He smelled wonderful, of soap and cologne. "Okay," she said, looking up. "I'll put the note in my desk, but I'm not going to think about it anymore."

"I'm glad." Todd's mouth skimmed her hair before he drew back. "Why don't we go see McMurdo Station and the penguins?" he invited.

Rachel's smile was tremulous. "Yes, why don't we. They're predicting a change in the weather, so I'd better get my windbreaker from the closet." She hated to leave the security of his arms.

"All right." Slowly, he released her. "But don't forget what I told you about your winter coat."

"I won't," she whispered, reaching to brush back a strand of his hair that had fallen onto his forehead. She could think of far worse things than being with Todd Andrews in "Antartica" with only one coat between them.

Chapter Five

After touring the zoo's exotic animal house and tropical aviary, Rachel and Todd spent the rest of the afternoon in the cavernous building that housed the Antarctic exhibit.

A guide led them through the mock-up of McMurdo Station, expounding on the rigors of arctic life for the scientists who conducted experiments at the South Pole.

"Those were pretty cramped quarters," Rachel remarked to Todd as they emerged from the station. "Especially for a place where the nights are six months long."

"It depends on who you're sharing them with." He grinned, taking hold of her hand as they strolled toward the penguin exhibit.

She had to concede Todd's point. In his company, spartan-looking McMurdo Station had taken on an aura of coziness. She decided the idea of living where one night lasted half the year might be very appealing under certain conditions. "Don't you feel as if you're actually in Antarctica?" she said at last.

He squeezed her hand in response. "If it was any more authentic I'd wonder why I didn't bring along a pair of mukluks."

Rachel's laughter bounced off the narrow corridor they'd just entered. At the other end was a sign that told them they had arrived at the "Polar Sea."

Todd whistled softly at the sight that greeted their eyes. Rachel drew in a sharp breath. Huge fake glaciers soared around them, so expertly crafted that they sparkled under the artificial sun, as actual ones might. The sea was a large expanse of water, clear and blue, where icebergs floated.

They stood, gaping, for a moment. Then Todd tugged at her arm. "Over there." He pointed to a slab of ice, real this time, that lay at the base of one of the glaciers. Clutches of penguins stood around its perimeter.

"I think penguins are the best thing about Antarctica," Rachel declared as she followed Todd to a spot right in front of the island of ice.

"They remind me of sea otters in certain ways," Todd announced after watching the animals frolic on the ice for a while.

Rachel glanced sideways at him. "Otters don't slide down glaciers on their bellies, do they?"

Todd returned her glance. "No, they slide down slippery hills and rocks on their backsides. There is another important difference too." His arm came around her waist.

"What's that?" She'd never been so fascinated by the subject of penguins, or otters, before.

"Otters look like they're having fun. Penguins look like they're on a business junket."

Rachel laughed. "You're right. Harried little men in stuffy suits. All that's missing are their tiny briefcases."

Todd chuckled, pulling her closer. She rested her head against his shoulder. Though he'd been joking about their winter coats, the temperature in this part of the exhibit was low enough to make her don her windbreaker and for him to put on the sweater he'd brought. But with his arm curved firmly about her waist again, Rachel was oblivious to the chill.

They watched in contented silence for a few more minutes. Consulting his watch, Todd said, "It's after five. Would you like to go or stay longer?"

"We can go, if you want." Though she'd been enjoying the penguins' antics, her attention was more focused on the man beside her.

As they exited the building, Rachel saw that the sky was black with clouds; it had begun to rain. Opting to skip the snack bar, they ran to the lot where Todd's car was parked.

They made it to the refuge of the Prelude just as the storm hit full force. Water streamed down the windows. Lightning flashed against the darkness and thunder shook the air like cannon fire.

Rachel started giggling. She couldn't help it. The pure pleasure of having spent the afternoon with Todd, the breathlessness that came with running to beat the rain, the fierceness of the deluge, all exhilarated her. One look at Todd told her he felt the same way.

"What?" he asked, though the question was redundant.

"It's nothing, only that I'm having a good time."

The crinkles around his eyes deepened and he reached over to wipe something from her brow. "I'm just returning a favor." He showed her his fingers.

They were wet with the determined raindrops that had pelted her before she slammed the car door shut. "Not mustard," she quipped.

His hand caught hers and drew her fingers to his chin.

"No, but I think I'm having a good time too." He leaned across the space that separated them. Then his lips met hers in a slow, sweet kiss.

She heard his sigh when he pulled back. His eyes lingered on her mouth as he asked, "Where would you like to have dinner, Rachel?"

Dare she tell him that her appetite had fled? Finally, she answered, "Spaghetti. I'm hungry for spaghetti. Don't ask me why."

Todd cupped her chin in his hand. "So spaghetti it is." He straightened and started the engine. Backing out of the parking space, he told her, "I know just the place. Becky used to waitress there."

Everyone must have known it was *the* place for spaghetti, Rachel thought, as they entered the tiny restaurant on the St. Paul side of the river. It was jammed; they were barely able to get in the front door.

Todd gave her a chagrined look. "It seems we're in for a long wait. Or we could go somewhere else."

The air was redolent with spicy smells. "You said this was the place for spaghetti. I wouldn't mind waiting." Rachel glanced around. There were no more than twenty tables and the line of people waiting for one appeared endless. Then she spotted a sign on the all. "Todd, they have carryout service."

He brightened. "You want your spaghetti to go?"

"Why not?" She had an idea. "We could take it home to my place. You wouldn't believe the great view from the balcony."

"Even in the rain?"

"It's better in the rain."

"I'll be right back." As he headed for the counter, he called to her over his shoulder, "Plain or meat sauce?"

"Whichever you like." She gave him an encouraging smile when he nearly knocked over a waiter carrying two huge pizzas.

While she waited for him, Rachel noted that the crowd seemed to be mostly U. of M. students. Defectors from the West Bank, she presumed. Someone bumped her arm. When she tried to see who it was, she got the strange feeling that she was being stared at.

Her eyes scanned the room—and met those of a tall young man standing not far away. He had short, curly dark hair and wore a university letter jacket. He wasn't bad looking, she decided, but the odd smile on his face sent a quiver through her. His smile, his whole attention, appeared focused on her.

Normally, she would ignore such a come-on and classify the guy as a jerk. But now she found herself staring back. Her hands sought the pockets of her windbreaker and balled into tight fists against the flimsy fabric.

"I'll be watching you." The words echoed in her mind. Absurd as it was, she had to wonder: was he the one who had sent the note to her? Who was he?

Rachel searched her memory for a clue as to the man's identity. Did she know him? Was he a former classmate who'd been at the reunion? It was hard to tell how old he was. He could be a university student. But the fact he wore a letter jacket didn't mean he currently attended the U. of M. Her eyes stayed locked with his as she tried to sort out anything familiar about his features. She came up blank. He was a complete stranger to her.

At that instant, a hand grasped her shoulder and she let out a small cry.

"Rachel?" Todd's face appeared in front of hers. "What's wrong?" He looked alarmed. "Did I scare you?"

She smiled weakly up at him. "No. It's . . . No, you didn't scare me." Wouldn't he think she was paranoid if she told him the truth?

Todd held a cardboard bucket with the word SPAGHETTI printed in large letters on its side. In his other hand was a smaller carton that she assumed was the sauce. He appeared skeptical about her reply, but all he said was, "Let's go then."

After they'd gotten into the car, Todd turned to her and covered her hand with his. "Rachel, what happened in there?"

She grimaced. "You'll think I'm silly."

"Never," he interrupted. His fingers gently stroked her wrist.

"I had a feeling that . . . I was being stared at. You know the feeling?" Todd shook his head. "There was someone, a man. I don't know who he was, but I thought of the anonymous note I'd received."

Todd looked disturbed. "It made you afraid?"

"Yes," she admitted. "Like I said earlier, I just want to forget the whole thing, not be paranoid over a dumb little message that must have been meant as a joke."

"You're not being paranoid. But, again, I think it's a good idea to treat the whole thing as a prank." Todd paused, then added quietly, "I'm not surprised that someone would stare at you, Rachel. You're a very beautiful woman."

His compliment took her by surprise; it flustered her. She'd never considered herself beautiful. Did Todd really think so? "Thank you," she said at last.

The way Todd's eyes caressed her face told her a change of subject was needed fast. "We'd better take our spaghetti home and eat it before it gets all gluey."

The ploy worked, but not before he placed a quick kiss on her mouth. "You have a way with words," he quipped as he started the car.

Rachel brought blankets and several large cushions out to the balcony for them to sit on while they ate. "I never got around to buying much stuff for the balcony," she explained as Todd spread the blankets in a corner and propped the cushions against the wall. The only other furniture was a small plastic table and a folding chair.

"There." Todd made a mock bow, inviting her to sit beside him. After they were settled, he ladled spaghetti and sauce onto the plates that she held out for him. They drank iced tea from gold-rimmed water goblets. She revealed the goblets were heirlooms handed down from her great-grandmother.

"My mother has a set of dishes that once belonged to her grandmother," Todd remarked. "She uses them only on special occasions, like her and Dad's thirtieth wedding anniversary last year."

Rachel glanced away; somehow the word "wedding" made her feel uncomfortable. She told herself she was being absurd. "Look," she said, pointing toward the small park that lay below them on the boulevard. "Don't the trees seem a deeper shade of green when they're wet? I love that view," she added. "Whenever there's a storm, I come out here."

"The view's fantastic," Todd agreed, but his eyes were on her, not the park.

Rachel occupied herself with her plate of spaghetti. After taking a bite, she dared a glance up at Todd. "This is delicious."

His head was bent over his heaped-up plate. "I was sure you'd like Nunzio's spaghetti," he replied. He raised his head to give Rachel a satisfied smile.

They ate in silence for a few minutes, taking sips from their goblets. Though the storm had passed, a steady drizzle had commenced, one that was apt to keep up all night.

"This is good sleeping weather," Todd said. He put his empty plate aside. "It reminds me of Seattle."

"It rains a lot there, doesn't it?" Rachel took a last bite of spaghetti, then set her plate next to Todd's.

"Sure does." He leaned back against the pillow and stretched his legs out on the blanket. "At first when I moved there, I missed the seasons."

"Seattle doesn't have seasons?"

"Not four like in St. Paul. There's the rainy season and then there's . . . the rainy season." He grinned. "I grew to love it anyway. The Pacific Northwest is green pretty much year-round; it looks like a rain forest. And the coast is great. Rugged and windy. It reminds me of the north shore of the lake."

Rachel knew he meant Lake Superior. "I enjoy going to the lake, but I always thought I'd like to live beside the ocean. How did you happen to choose Seattle, though?" She immediately wondered if it had been Stacey's idea.

"I'd gone there on an interview just before I was to graduate from Cal State. A small property development company invited me up. They'd just landed a choice contract with the city of Seattle." Todd gazed in the direction of the park. "They made me a good offer."

He hadn't mentioned Stacey. Rachel noticed in a detached way that the streetlights below had come on. The pavement shimmered in the growing darkness. But when she looked at Todd, she saw something else that glistened. His eyes, lowered, fringed by golden lashes, were not quite hidden from her in the faint light.

"Are you sure you're over Stacey?" The softly worded question sounded unnaturally loud in the secluded setting of the balcony.

Todd raised his eyes to meet hers and she couldn't doubt the answer he gave. "I'm positive, Rachel." His voice, equally soft, was firm. "Come here," he said a little gruffly, reaching for her.

She went to him, perhaps too eagerly, and nestled herself within the crook of his arm.

"Are *you* sure? Are you over Jeff?"

Though his words sounded almost teasing, the mention of Jeff's name made Rachel tremble. She wasn't sure why. Nor could she say why it was so difficult to answer Todd, even if her memories of Jeff now were painful ones.

Todd cleared his throat. "I had just about worked up the courage to ask you out when you started going with Jeff."

"I . . . I wish you had." Her response caused Todd's arm to tighten around her. Mickey had been right. And hadn't Meg also guessed that Todd must have had a crush on the girl he'd enjoyed teasing?

"Of course that was when I was only dazzled by your beauty," he said almost lightly. "Before I understood my feelings for you were far more serious than that."

Rachel turned so that they were face-to-face. "But didn't you love Stacey?"

Todd averted his eyes. "After a while I convinced myself that I did." His eyes came back to search hers. "My heart obviously knew better."

Rachel swallowed hard. "If only I'd known," she said finally. The wistful confession did nothing to ease the tension building between them.

But the thought that entered her mind, the odd sensation that accompanied it, made her realize why she'd reacted in the way she had to the mention of Jeff's name. Rachel sat up straight. "Jeff. He could be the one." She said it more to herself than to Todd.

"What do you mean?"

"The note." She gripped Todd's arm. "Jeff must have sent it. He was watching me while we were dancing. You saw him, didn't you?"

The tension between them was gone, replaced by a different sort of strain. Todd raked a hand through his hair. "That's why I led you to the other side of the room.

I guessed you were upset because you saw him standing there. I wasn't aware that he was watching you.''

"I'd never considered that Jeff had a sense of humor. But apparently he does.'' Rachel waited for Todd's affirmation that she was on the right track.

"Why would he do that to you?'' Todd sounded uncertain himself as his arm came back around her. He drew her close and she brought her hand up to lie against his sweater. She could feel the rise and fall of his chest. "We can't be sure Jeff sent the note,'' Todd cautioned after a moment.

"I can't imagine who else it might be.''

"You'd told me that Jeff became a doctor. What kind of doctor, Rachel?''

The look on her face must have betrayed her, for Todd frowned in response. "A pathologist. With the Ramsey County coroner's office.''

"Right here in St. Paul.'' With one hand, Todd picked up his goblet. His other hand stayed firmly at her back. He held the nearly empty glass in front of them. Illumination from a lamp inside shone through the liquid. Todd drank the last swallows of tea and set the glass down.

"If you remember,'' Rachel said quietly, "Jeff liked working with dead bodies.'' It was her own vain attempt to make light of the subject.

Todd's reaction was swift. His arms locked around her waist. "Rachel—'' He stopped short.

She gazed up at him. "Would you like some more tea?''

"Not now. What I'd like is for you to be careful. Not afraid, just careful,'' he emphasized.

"All right.'' The promise seemed easy to make, here in the security of his embrace. He projected strength, and an aura of such pure protectiveness that the breath caught in Rachel's throat. As his eyes moved over her face, she found herself longing for a kiss.

He must have known, for he brought his mouth to hers. The kiss was tenderly possessive. When it ended, they sat silently, foreheads touching.

Finally, he moved away a fraction. "That drink you offered me. I could use a little."

"I'll have some too."

Todd withdrew his arms from around her to retrieve the carafe of iced tea. She held the goblets again while he poured.

As they sipped, Rachel took advantage of the subtle shift in mood to change the subject. "Tell me about your work on the Kilborn project. Silverthorne must have been very impressed with you." She immediately wondered why she had chosen a topic only slightly less disturbing than the one they'd been discussing.

Todd gazed out over the balcony. "I think it might have been more the other way around. I was impressed with Silverthorne. So much so that I did my best to land a job with them."

His answer didn't bring Rachel any comfort. She studied his profile, the finely chiseled set of his jaw. "How did you find out about the position?"

"They ran an ad in the *Seattle Times*." Todd directed his smile at her. "I sent my résumé in and two weeks later Bradley Silverthorne called me for an interview. One week after that he made me an offer."

"It all happened very fast."

"Yes, but remember what I told you at the reunion? That you were the reason I came back?"

"But you believed I was married to Jeff. You told me that too."

"That's what I thought. My heart hoped differently."

"Your heart was right."

"I should have listened to it long ago," he declared, taking her goblet from her hand to set it alongside his.

As he framed her face in his hands, drawing her near, Rachel had the impression that she was falling. Was it the electricity-charged air after the storm that made her feel that way, or was it the dizzying speed with which Todd was courting her? Just before his lips covered hers, Meg's warning spun through her mind: *Todd Andrews is a dangerously handsome man.*

"I've got to go," Todd said huskily when their lips parted. He rose to leave. He helped her up, but didn't touch her again as they walked through the living room to the front door.

He hesitated, turning to her as if he would kiss her once more. Instead, he put a hand on her shoulder. "What are your hours at the boutique on Saturdays?"

"Noon until six. Why?" she asked expectantly.

Todd smiled. "Because I wanted to ask if you'd have dinner with me next Saturday evening, maybe take in a movie too." He explained that Silverthorne was sending him to Chicago for a seminar. He wouldn't be back in town until late Friday.

Rachel suspected the expression on her face matched the look of chagrin on his. It seemed he was no more eager to go to Chicago than she was to see him go.

Yet she argued with herself that it would be good for them both. With Todd at a distance, she might be able to more rationally examine what was happening between them. He would have the same chance.

"I'd love to have dinner with you on Saturday." She tried not to sound too anxious.

"Good." He looked at her with longing as if he wanted to say more. But all he told her as he started out the door was, "Remember, Rachel, take care."

She wanted to tell him that she missed him already.

What came out was, "You take care too, Todd," as she stared after him.

Rachel's fingers fumbled when she tried to call Sue, causing her to dial a wrong number.

Relax, she told herself as she dialed again. The admonition did little good. The sound of Sue's voice on the other end almost caused Rachel to hang up. *Chicken,* she scolded herself. *But then how do I begin to tell a very dear and old friend that I'm falling in love with the man she's wanted for years?*

"Hello?" Sue repeated.

"I'm sorry, Sue. It's Rachel." There—at least she'd gotten a couple of words out.

"Oh, hi, Rachel."

The greeting was cool, Rachel noted—or did she just imagine that it was? "I hope I didn't catch you at a bad time, Sue."

"No." There was a brief silence. "Well, actually, I am kind of busy."

"I'm sorry." Rachel experienced a small rush of relief. But postponing the matter would do nothing to quell the reason for her anxiety. "Would it be better if I call back later, or do you want to phone me when it's convenient?" How stiffly formal her own voice sounded, as though she were talking to someone she barely knew.

There was another pause. "I can talk for just a minute or two now."

That would be enough, Rachel decided. "The reason I called was to ask if you'd like to get together for lunch sometime in the next few days. Whenever's best for you," she added.

Sue's reply was swift. "I'd love to, Rachel, but I'm afraid I won't have a minute to spare the whole week. The district manager of Europa Spas will be in town. There'll be meetings, meetings, meetings. Some other time? You know, Diane's coming back in a few weeks, and Mickey said she'd like to get together too.''

"Why don't we plan on the four of us having lunch then, as we agreed at the reunion.''

"Great!'' Sue sounded excited for the first time in their short conversation. "I've got to run, but I'll call you when I hear from Diane.''

There was a click as Sue hung up the phone on her end. Rachel slowly lowered the receiver to its cradle, feeling more troubled than she had before the conversation. At the reunion she'd been enthusiastic about the four friends meeting for lunch; now she wished it could be just she and Sue. Diane and Mickey's company would hardly lend itself to an intimate discussion of who was in love with Todd and what was to be done about it. Maybe she could ask Sue for a private tour of the spa or invite her over for pizza some evening, just the two of them. Then they could talk privately.

Rachel sighed. She'd intended to call Meg tonight too. She wasn't in the mood anymore. Instead, she switched on her answering machine and decided that a hot bath was what she needed. The air had turned cool in the evening. Was that what made the apartment feel uncomfortably drafty?

In any case, a good soak should ease the knot of tension that had suddenly formed at the back of her neck. She could attempt to read another chapter in that boring historical novel she'd bought on a whim at the bookstore last week. If the warm water didn't make her sleepy, the dirgelike slowness of the story might. And sleep would be sure to banish the terrible emptiness she'd felt since Todd had left for Chicago.

The next afternoon Meg came rushing into the boutique. She was wearing the purple pantsuit. Today, it looked slightly wrinkled. "I can only stay a minute,'' she said, catching her breath. "I'm meeting Phil uptown in half an hour, but I wanted to check in and see when we could get together." She gulped in another breath.

Rachel had to smile. Meg was notorious for running late, especially where her boyfriend and her friends were concerned. "You're stunning in that suit, you know, even if a bit rumpled today."

Meg seemed to notice her appearance for the first time. "That's what Phil said when I modeled the suit for him. That is, the stunning part." She paused, frowning. "Oh, I do look rumpled!"

"But beautifully so." Rachel hid a yawn.

Meg regarded her with interest. "So, has the handsome hunk been depriving you of your beauty sleep?"

"Handsome hunk?" Rachel said innocently, though the reference conjured up pleasant images in her mind and caused an ache in the vicinity of her heart.

Meg waved her hand. "Now, Rach, who else but Todd Andrews would keep you out past your bedtime these days? I tried to call you last night and got your answering machine," she added in a mock accusing tone. "Wait! What are these?" She took a step closer. "Circles under your eyes?"

Rachel turned her head. "I didn't check my messages this morning," she admitted, hoping Meg would take the hint and let the subject drop.

She didn't. "What's the matter, Rach? I was just teasing, you know."

"I know." The reply was too tentative, a little melancholy. Rachel felt Meg's eyes on her. "Todd's out of town this week. And I miss him . . . a lot," she confessed, turning back to her friend.

"Of course you do," Meg quickly commiserated. She looked thoughtful. "But isn't this all happening awfully fast? I mean—" She shrugged. "Do you honestly feel you're falling in love with the man?"

If anyone else had asked the question, Rachel might have snapped that it really was none of her business. But this was Meg and she'd long ago accepted her friend's forthrightness. It also happened that Meg had lent Rachel her unquestioning support after the nasty split with Jeff. "I honestly feel that I am," Rachel said at last. "It's not as if Todd's a stranger I just met."

Meg's eyes locked with hers. "That's true, but people do change, Rach." She paused, looking away. "Are you sure you know him so well after ten years?"

Rachel's defenses rose. "If there's been any change in Todd, it's for the better. I'm positive of that," she added stubbornly.

Meg's hand grasped hers. "I'm sorry. I realize I sound like an uncaring shrew and you're already convinced I don't like Todd. I swear it's not true," Hesitating, she said in a whisper, "I just don't want to see you get stung again."

Rachel flung her arms around her friend. "Oh, Meg, I need to talk. It's not Todd himself. He's absolutely wonderful. But there are other things . . . much too complicated to tell you about now." Her eyes misted. "Phil's waiting and you're going to be late."

Meg regarded Rachel for a moment. "You said Todd's out of town. Does that include Friday?" Rachel nodded. "Well, it just happens that Phil has a big project due next Monday and he'll be working late, *way late*, Friday," she emphasized. "Why don't we have dinner together, maybe take in one of those soppy, ten-tissue movies afterwards? I understand there's a new one at the Mercury that's guaranteed to make us cry into our popcorn."

A laugh that sounded more like a hiccup escaped from Rachel. "I've got an even better idea. Would you believe that *Wuthering Heights* is playing on the classic movie channel? We could go back to my apartment and lounge in front of the TV with a box of tissues and a huge chocolate-chip cheesecake.''

Meg's eyes lit up. ''Yes! But only if the cheesecake is from Bentley's.''

''Agreed.'' Bentley's had a reputation for making the most sinfully rich desserts in town.

''Then it'll be pure heaven.'' Meg grinned. ''I can't wait for Friday.''

''Neither can I.'' For the first time in days, Rachel found herself looking forward to something.

''And after we've had a good cry over the trials of poor Cathy and Heathcliff, we can hash over whatever's complicating your life at the moment.''

''It's a deal.'' Rachel hugged her friend.

Meg promised to call Thursday evening so they could decide where to have dinner. Then she made a dash for the door. Looking back over her shoulder, she admonished, ''Be sure to get some sleep tonight, Rach.''

Despite Meg's good advice, Rachel suspected that sleep would be elusive. Maybe if she hadn't turned on her answering machine the moment she'd gotten home and heard Todd's voice on the tape, she could have settled down early to a decent night's rest.

But his message echoed in her mind long after she'd listened to it. And how could she help playing his unexpected call over at least five times? *''I had to phone. I miss you so much, Rachel. I wanted to hear your voice. . . . Despite what the calendar says about the seasons, Chicago is blustery and cold, much too cold without you in my arms.''*

The words sounded like poetry to her ears, yet they made her feel cold too. Hadn't he just read lines from Shakespeare with the same intensity? A tremor coursed through Rachel. The mysterious, unsigned note was one of the things she wanted to discuss with Meg. She was becoming more and more convinced that Jeff was the sender.

But, at the moment, she wanted only to relish the warm rush of feeling she'd gotten from Todd's call. At the end, he'd promised to contact her Saturday morning. That made her smile, even if he'd just managed to derail her plans to examine their relationship in a rational light while he was away.

As she prepared for bed later, she was hopeful that whatever sleep she might steal would include dreams of Todd. She couldn't ask for anything sweeter.

Chapter Six

Any dreams Rachel might have had of Todd were tempered by more troubling ones, though she could remember only snatches of them. What she was certain of was that Jeff had been in them. And that was enough to make her uneasy, to cause her to cast a glance around her when she left her apartment building the next morning for Cabbage Rose's.

With time, and her mind set on her customers and the weekly inventory and receiving of new consignments, Rachel's uneasiness diminished.

But on Friday the disquiet returned with a ferocity she hadn't known before. It began after she closed the boutique an hour early so that she could rush home and change clothes for her dinner date with Meg. They'd decided to meet at a posh yet cozy German restaurant not far from Rachel's apartment building.

As Rachel joined the pedestrian traffic outside Penny Lane, she had the sudden sensation that someone's eyes were on her. It was the same eerie awareness that she'd experienced the night she and Todd had stopped for spaghetti.

Jostled and propelled forward by the sheer volume of people, she scanned the crowd as best she could. She recognized none of the faces around her and didn't see the one she might have expected to. Everyone was a stranger—and none seemed to be paying her the least attention.

Still, the feeling followed her to Bentley's, two blocks up, where she purchased the cheesecake, then again to the parking garage where she had a year-round pass to park her car.

If it had been later when the garage was nearly empty, she would have been frightened, though constant glances over her shoulder turned up no sign of anyone even remotely familiar.

But after she'd arrived at her building and stopped to check her mailbox in the foyer, a numbing thought entered her mind. Had the idea that she was being watched been triggered by her subconscious? For in her box was just one piece of mail, a business-size envelope with her name and address typed neatly on the outside. There was no return address.

Hands shaking, Rachel removed the envelope, fingering it gingerly as if it might burn her. On Friday a week ago the first anonymous message had come. And now it was Friday again.

She headed quickly for the elevator and punched the button for her floor. It seemed an eternity until the elevator came.

There was no one else inside the cubicle as she rode to the eighth floor. When the elevator doors quietly slid open, she almost ran down the deserted corridor to her apartment. Letting herself in, she tossed her purse aside on the sofa.

For several minutes Rachel held the envelope in her hands, not moving. Then she took a deep breath and tore open the flap. As had happened before, a folded piece of paper fell out.

She unfolded it, clutching it in her fingers. She read the words typed in the center of the page.

> *And trouble deaf heaven with my bootless cries,*
> *And look upon myself, and curse my fate. . . . "*

She knew they had to be the next lines of the Shakespeare poem. She read on:

> *Do you know the lines now, Rachel? You were with*
> *him last weekend, weren't you? Did he kiss you?*
> *Did he make you happy? You can't get away from*
> *me, Rachel. This is a warning! Be careful! I'LL BE*
> *WATCHING YOU . . . AND WAITING.*

Rachel gasped for air. "No!" she cried softly. "Why? Why are you doing this, Jeff?" It was so unfair that now, just when the future seemed so full of promise, he would conspire to spoil it. But hadn't that been his pattern, especially in the last months of their relationship? And even if he hadn't been a part of her life recently, no doubt he had just been waiting for another chance.

She felt like a wreck, but she had to get dressed and be on her way if she hoped to meet Meg on time. There would be no possibility of deceiving Meg, of course, even with a fresh change of clothes and application of makeup. Besides, she had no appetite for dinner. Not even chocolate-chip cheesecake sounded appealing tonight.

Moving to the kitchen, Rachel set the cheesecake in the refrigerator. Then she went to her desk, opened the drawer, and took out the note she had stashed there on

Todd's advice. She put the two notes together and stuffed them into her purse, afraid that what she had to tell Meg would ruin her friend's appetite too.

"How can you be so sure Jeff sent these?" Meg indicated the notes spread out on the table before her. She reached over to cover Rachel's hand with her own for an instant. "I didn't say that quite right. I can understand why you would think it has to be him. But are—" Meg shook her head. "Could there be other possibilities, Rach? You said this first note came after the reunion and that these lines are the ones you recited at a Shakespeare festival."

Rachel gave her friend a tired smile. "You sound like Todd. But I just can't imagine who else would want to send me something like . . . like that." She slumped back against the booth they were sitting in. At least she could take consolation in the fact she'd managed to keep from ruining Meg's meal. Putting on a chipper front, she'd chatted about a fabulous new batch of clothing that had come into the store. All the while Meg was busy devouring her sauerbraten and potato dumplings.

Only when Meg was nearly done with her meal did she lay down her fork and look Rachel pointedly in the eye. "You can quit being the actress now," she'd said without a smile. "You've won the Academy Award already, but your plate is a dead giveaway," she'd added to Rachel's shaky laugh.

Meg toyed with her water glass before taking a careful sip. Then she leaned toward Rachel over the table. "Can you think of anyone besides Jeff who might want to upset you?"

Rachel straightened. Another smile crossed her lips. "At first I thought it was Todd." She looked at Meg.

"Because he's a tease?"

"No. Because he'd told me at the reunion that he'd been watching me all evening."

Meg's eyebrows rose. "Oh, well, that figures. But obviously, it wasn't him."

Rachel shook her head. She put her fingers to her temples and tried to massage away the beginnings of a headache. Shutting her eyes, an image unexpectedly appeared behind the closed lids. "Sidney," she said, gasping.

"What?"

Rachel's eyes grew wide. "Sidney Wetherly! You asked if someone else could have sent the notes," she explained, feeling triumphant for having thought of another possibility, however remote, besides Jeff.

"But who is Sidney Wetherly?"

"I could show you. In the *Windjammer*."

"Your high school yearbook!" Meg sounded excited too. "What are we waiting for? Let's go back to your apartment. We're going to play detective, Rach."

"Yours first. And Todd's too," Meg declared as Rachel flipped through the book they held between them on the sofa.

"Okay," Rachel said grudgingly, though she was only teasing. "I guess you've waited long enough." She turned to the page where their pictures were, hers above his.

"Very cute," Meg pronounced after studying the photos for a moment. "Even then, you looked like you were made for each other. Now let's see this Sidney guy."

Made for each other. The words echoed in Rachel's mind as she turned the several pages to Sidney's photo.

Meg studied it. "I know someone like him. But don't most people?" She smiled, but then her face took on a more serious expression. "It could be him, Rach."

"I don't know," Rachel hedged. On the way out of the restaurant she'd clued Meg in on Sidney's seeming

obsession with her in high school and her strange encounter with him at the reunion. "My intuition still tells
me that it has to be Jeff."

"But Sidney did ask you to dance and declared that
you'd get tired of Todd and think of him. The man
sounds like he doesn't have all his oars in the water."

Rachel smiled wanly at her friend. "No, I don't think
he does." She went back a few pages in the *Windjammer.* "It's funny. In some ways, Sidney used to remind
me of Mickey."

"I recall you mentioning her name. So, who's
Mickey?"

"But what about *Wuthering Heights?*" Checking her
watch, Rachel saw that it was almost time for the movie
to start.

Meg waved her hand. "Oh, forget *Wuthering Heights*
for tonight. This is far more interesting than watching an
old movie, even it if is one of our favorites. Tell me
about Mickey . . . and Sue. I remember you mentioned
her too. Tell me about everyone." She flung her arms
in an expansive gesture. "Maybe we can dig up more
suspects."

Rachel laughed, reaching to squeeze Meg's fingers.
"I'm so glad you're here, Sherlock."

"I guess that makes you Watson," her friend shot
back with a grin. "So, Watson, clue me in on Mickey."

"There. Michaela Franklin. As long as I can remember, though, everyone called her Mickey." Rachel
pointed to the appropriate photo. "She doesn't look anything like that now."

"Really?" Meg regarded Rachel with curiosity.

"Uh-uh. In fact, I barely recognized her at the reunion. Sometime in the last ten years, she lost all the excess
weight." Rachel covered the photo with her hand.
"She's gorgeous, Meg, but I don't think she realizes it."

"I'd like to meet Mickey."

"I'm sure you'll get to someday, now that I'm back in touch with her." Rachel paused, thoughtful. "In school, Mickey didn't fit in, of course. Like Sidney," she explained. "Sue, Diane, and I kind of took Mickey into our group and made her our project."

"Diane?"

"She was the fourth member of our little band of friends. Super outgoing, popular. She's married to a stockbroker and lives in New York City." Rachel noted that Meg looked duly impressed. "I'll show you her picture. But getting back to Mickey, we tried to make her feel part of us. I used to imagine we were helping her."

"Did she resent it?" Meg asked, ever intuitive.

Rachel frowned. "I'm beginning to think so. I took on the role of Mickey's protector when the other kids made fun of her. I never considered she might resent my help."

"You were her self-appointed bodyguard," Meg rejoined. "I can see you in that role."

Rachel gave her friend a rueful smile. "I suppose I was. At the reunion, I was surprised that she still had the same defensive air about her as in the past. I'm sure it was her way of keeping the hurt out."

Studying Mickey's unsmiling photo, Rachel continued, "I'd always thought that she was edgy because of her weight, but when Rob Ransom made a play for her at the reunion, she acted like she couldn't stand him. She called him a bore. It was the kind of response I would have expected from her in high school."

"Maybe the man is a bore." Meg paused. "Or maybe Mickey's simply suspicious because she doesn't consider herself attractive."

"I wonder what she sees when she looks in the mirror."

"Not *what,* but *who,* Rach. A woman she hasn't come to terms with yet."

"You're probably right." The talk about Mickey brought Sue to Rachel's mind. She turned to her photo. "That's Sue?"

"Yes. And it seems she's been losing weight too."

Meg studied the photo closely. "Sue doesn't appear heavy. She looks fragile, I'd say."

"You're right." Rachel met Meg's eyes. "Sue was one of the things I wanted to discuss with you."

"Go on, but why do I have a feeling this has to do with Todd?"

Rachel gave an ironic laugh. "Because it does. Remember I'd told you that Sue liked Todd in high school? *More* than liked. I'm positive she still does."

"Is Todd aware that two women, very good friends at that, are madly in love with him?"

Rachel cast Meg a withering glance. "Make that three women." Meg's eyes widened appropriately. "But woman number three could hardly be considered a friend."

"The plot thickens."

"Yes, but first about Sue. The problem is, I don't know how to broach the subject with her. Especially when I'm afraid Sue already has some difficulties of her own."

"Like what?" Meg probed.

"Anorexia."

Meg sucked in a sharp breath. "That is bad, Rach, but how can you be sure she's anorexic? Some people are just naturally thin."

"She was thin enough for me to be alarmed, Meg. Besides, at the reunion, she barely ate a bite from her plate, even though it was piled with food."

"It might have been nerves."

"There you go again."

Meg held up a hand. "You know what *your* problem is?"

Rachel gave her friend a knowing glance. "My problem is I'm afraid to approach Sue about Todd."

Meg shook her head. "Uh-uh. Your problem is that you're too noble."

Rachel was taken aback. "Why do you say that?"

"Because you're trying to figure out a way to play fair, to be loyal to both a very good friend and the man you're falling head over heels for."

"What's wrong with playing fair?" Rachel retorted.

Meg's eyebrows rose. "Nothing, except that it's raising havoc with your emotions."

Rachel fell silent. Meg's hand touched her arm.

"Why don't you ask Sue to come over to Cabbage Rose's, tell her you've got a couple of outfits you'd like for her to try on. You could talk to her then."

Despite her irritation over Meg's remarks, Rachel had to admit it was a good suggestion. "Maybe I'll do that," she said at last.

Meg didn't seem to hear. Her mood grew suddenly somber as she grabbed hold of Rachel's arm. "Sue! You don't suppose. . . . " Meg's face wore an anxious expression. "I realize it seems unlikely, but Sue apparently has this thing for Todd and the notes started coming after the reunion—"

"You believe that *Sue* could be the one?" Rachel interrupted. She looked at Meg, incredulous. "How could you even think such a thing?"

Meg appeared contrite, but "I'm sorry," was all she said.

They fell into an uneasy silence, neither looking at the other. Finally, Rachel reached for Meg's hand. "You don't have to apologize. We're supposed to be considering the possibilities. It's just that you tell me I'm being noble. Then you bring up the idea that Sue might be the stalker."

The word, once voiced, seem to hang in the air. It sent

a quiver of fear through Rachel. "It can't be Sue," she went on, the words choked. "Besides, the stalker wouldn't be a woman."

"Why not? Do you think only men are stalkers?"

Rachel searched for a reply. "I guess what I mean is that if someone is watching me, it makes more sense to me that it would be a man. Jeff," she added with a note of defiance. "I think he's just being cruel."

"Don't forget Sidney," Meg reminded quietly. "In fact, Rach, I think it would be a good idea to make a list."

Rachel gave a sigh of resignation. "All right. I'll get a pad and pen." She rose, feeling numb, and went over to the desk. She located the writing materials in a drawer. "Wait," she called to Meg. "We need something else."

Retreating to the bedroom, she returned with her souvenir book and showed it to Meg. "Whoever sent the notes must still live around the Twin Cities. The envelopes had a St. Paul postmark. Jeff lives here, of course. And Sue," she added reluctantly.

Meg took the tablet and pen. "What about Sidney?"

Rachel searched through the book and located his name. "Yes. 1482 West 34th St., St. Paul," she read off.

"Not exactly uptown," Meg remarked.

"No." In fact, West 34th Street was in a particularly seedy part of the city. "It's strange because his parents are rich. Listen. Sidney's occupation is a cabdriver."

Meg recorded the information. "That means he gets around a lot." Looking up, she said, "What about this third woman in the Todd Andrews' love triangle?"

Rachel laughed at the reference, but her sense of humor soon fled. "Kerrie Bowles." Briefly, she told Meg about Kerrie's determination to snare Todd. "She couldn't be the stalker."

"Why not?"

"Because she's a model in New York City." Rachel felt a little smug.

"How do you know?"

"I found out at the reunion. Here." Rachel singled out Kerrie's picture. "What do you think?"

"Definitely the model type," Meg agreed, studying the likeness.

Rachel next found Kerrie's name in the souvenir book. "See, it says—" She stopped short.

Meg took the book from her hands. "It says that Kerrie's address is 28 Perry Plaza in the fine city of St. Paul. You were right about the model part, Rach, except Kerrie left New York to take a job with the Browne Agency in Minneapolis." She bent over the tablet.

"What are you writing?"

"Just the facts, ma'am," Meg said with a wink.

The friends spent the next couple of hours perusing the *Windjammer* and the souvenir book. They looked at more photographs with Rachel supplying the reminiscences. And they uncovered the sometimes startling directions her former classmates' lives had taken.

In between they ate two slices apiece of cheesecake. Feeling stuffed, Rachel conceded that she'd more than made up for her lack of enthusiasm at dinner.

She credited her reawakened appetite to Meg and the notion that she was beginning to put the matter of the mysterious notes into perspective.

After all, she and Meg had been able to come up with no more than four names on their list of possible suspects—Jeff, Sidney, Sue, and Kerrie, only one of which she could consider seriously. It was that one, though, that left her with a lingering sense of uneasiness that she couldn't cast off.

When Meg rose to leave, Rachel found herself asking, "Do you have to go just yet?"

"I wish I could stay longer, Rach. But I've got to be in the office at seven tomorrow." Meg covered a yawn with the back of her hand. "There's a mountain of paperwork on my desk." She made a face. "And a meeting at nine."

"On Saturday?"

"The board of realtors shows no mercy." Meg gave Rachel a hug at the door. "You'll be fine. You'll see Todd tomorrow."

"True," Rachel admitted in as restrained a manner as possible. In reality, she could hardly wait for morning and his phone call.

Meg regarded her for a moment. "Let me know if you get any more notes, Rach. Be alert. Not frightened," she added hastily.

"You and Todd agree on that."

Meg smiled, but let the remark pass. "We may have come up with only four names, but remember that it could be almost anyone who attended the reunion." The concern in her eyes was unmistakable.

"Anyone who has a long memory of my performance at the Elizabethan Festival *and* who lives in or about St. Paul."

"Well, that does narrow the field a bit." Meg laughed. It sounded forced. She turned and left, waving back at Rachel before entering the elevator.

Rachel stared down the empty hallway for a moment. Then she closed her door and locked it. Though she heard the deadbolt slide into place, she checked the lock twice to make certain it was secure.

She looked at the time. It was nearly midnight. She wished she felt sleepy instead of wide awake. Opening the balcony doors, she stepped outside. A harsh gust of wind blew around the corner of the balcony. It made her think of Todd's call. *"Chicago is blustery and cold . . . much too cold without you in my arms."*

"So is St. Paul," Rachel whispered into the air. She gazed at the array of lights along the boulevard. The dark patch of the park was the only break in the twinkling chain. Shivering, Rachel retreated to the warmth of her living room.

She went over and turned on the TV, thinking she might catch and old movie. Curling up on the sofa, Rachel flipped through the channels. The only choices seemed to be home shopping networks and a couple of tabloid news shows. She opted for one of the tabloid programs, though she had a distaste for them.

"Police today found the body of Broadway actress Flora Gonzales in an alleyway adjacent to the Fenton Theater," a reporter announced. A picture of the star flashed on the screen. "An apparent victim of a brutal homicide, Ms. Gonzales had been stabbed repeatedly. Just last week, the star of the revival of the hit musical *West Side Story* had filed a complaint against a fan whom she claimed had been stalking her."

Suddenly, Rachel came to attention; her hand gripped the remote control. The rest of the report said that a suspect had been brought in and quickly released for lack of evidence. Then the show went to a commercial break. Her head reeled, replaying the reporter's words. Many times she had heard or read about people being stalked. But never before had any report caused such terror as she knew at that moment.

That could be me, she thought, envisioning the beautiful star lying lifeless in a bleak, dirty alleyway. *Don't be silly,* her mind countered. *Someone just wants to frighten you, not kill you.*

Rachel wasn't convinced, though she kept repeating the reassurance to herself as she turned off the TV and crossed into the bedroom. Getting ready for bed, she considered how the search for suspects had seemed almost like a game in Meg's company. Now the game had taken on a sinister tone and all Rachel knew to do was wait for the stalker to make his next move.

It was midnight. The moonless sky told her so. She was walking down the boulevard away from her building. There was no one else on the street, no traffic. No one but him. She knew he was there, in the shadows of the park, silently, stealthily waiting for her.

His eyes, coldly calculating, hot with anger, were on her. She came closer, his notes clutched in her hand. All at once, he was in front of her, darker and more foreboding than the blackness surrounding him. She tried to scream, but all that came out was a whisper. "Jeff!"

A sound like an alarm wakened her. Groggily, Rachel reached to turn off the alarm clock by her bed. The noise didn't stop. Finally, she realized the ringing came from the phone.

Picking up the receiver, Rachel saw that bright shafts of sunlight shone through the cracks in the window blinds. But she'd been dreaming that it was night.

"Todd!" she mumbled, fighting the sense of confusion that enveloped her. "Hello?" she said into the mouthpiece. The word came out more as a rasp.

"Rachel?"

His voice chased away the chill in her bones. Her eyes moved to the alarm clock again, registering the time. Nine-thirty. "I'm sorry, Todd. I overslept."

"Are you all right?"

How was he able to instantly sense when something was wrong? Rachel sighed. "Not exactly. I had a dream. A bad one," she confessed, remembering the nightmare.

She heard Todd draw a sharp breath. "Then I'm coming over." There was a second of silence. "I need to see you, Rachel." Another pause. "And I think you need to see me."

He had no idea how much she craved to see him, but

panic began to set in. She was still in bed, barely awake. All she could say was, "Coming over? Now?"

"Yes. That is . . . " He cleared his throat. "I apologize this time. You have to be in the store at noon."

"It's early yet," she said eagerly, hoping he wouldn't change his mind. "Just let me get dressed. I want you to come, Todd," she whispered.

"How about fifteen minutes?" he whispered back.

"Perfect." She got out of bed, still holding the phone.

"I'm on my way," Todd replied, then hung up.

Rachel would never have imagined she could move as fast as she did, especially without that first vital cup of coffee she always had in the morning. But she managed to take a five-minute shower, pull on a fresh pair of jeans and a blouse, dash on a touch of mascara and lipstick, and brush her hair into a semblance of order before Todd came.

As soon as she opened the door and saw Todd standing there, Rachel flung herself into his waiting arms. He held her tightly, uttering words into her ear that she couldn't quite hear. Yet she understood them perfectly. Tilting her head, she murmured his name. His lips met hers in a kiss that more than made up for his absence.

"I got your phone call," she said when he drew back from her. "Was it really that bad in Chicago?"

"Miserable," he whispered before kissing her again.

Tearing herself from him, Rachel motioned for Todd to follow her. She led him to the sofa and they sat down together. He was dressed casually too, she noted, in jeans and a cotton shirt whose blue shade made him look even more dazzling than usual. Or did it only seem that way because she'd missed him terribly?

"I just want to look at you," Todd said after a moment. It was a redundant statement; his gaze hadn't left her face since he'd arrived.

Rachel's skin grew warm under the caress of his eyes.

And the cologne he was wearing pleased another of her senses. "Um. What's that?" she asked, touching his cheek.

"What?" His eyes crinkled at the corners.

"Your cologne."

"Oh. I'm glad you like it. It's called Risk. I picked it up in Chicago." He reached in his jeans pocket and pulled out an oblong white box tied with a gold ribbon. "And I picked this up for you, Rachel."

She looked at him, surprised, as he pressed the gift into her hand. "Oh, Todd. . . . "

"Open it," he urged.

She did, fingers trembling a little. Lifting the lid on the box, she found a necklace nestled inside. It was one of the loveliest pieces of jewelry she'd seen in some time, a fine gold chain intertwined with several strands of seed pearls. She took the piece out.

"What do you think?" he asked a bit anxiously.

The thought entered her mind that the gift must have cost a small fortune. Little wonder he would choose to wear a cologne named Risk. "The necklace is beautiful," she said aloud, meeting his eyes. "I don't know what to say, Todd, except . . . thank you."

He smiled as he took the necklace from her and carefully placed it around her neck. She bent forward so that he could fasten the clasp. "A beautiful necklace for a beautiful woman," he declared when he finished the task.

Too much, too fast, a cautious voice warned in some dim corner of Rachel's mind. But her heart dismissed the warning. She fingered the necklace, pleased with it, pleased with Todd's compliments too, and his nearness.

Finally, he said, "There was something I wanted to ask you."

"Yes?"

"Would you be willing to come home for dinner tonight instead of going out?'' He gave her a rueful smile. ''What I mean is, I want you to come over to my parents' house. They're anxious to see you, Rachel. It's been a while. Besides, Mom's been looking for another excuse to break out the good china.'' He smoothed one hand over his hair in a tentative gesture.

The request was one Rachel didn't have to think long about. ''That would be great, Todd.'' She'd always been fond of his parents, but then she hadn't been dating their son. Their relationship had been strictly an informal one. She knew tonight would be different, and it caused a nervous twinge in her stomach.

''Don't worry,'' Todd said close to her ear, as though he'd read her mind. ''They already love you too.''

Rachel started to smile, but the smile froze when she saw Todd's expression had turned serious. Intuitively, she knew what was coming.

He reached for her hand. ''Tell me about the dream that upset you.'' Pausing, he added, ''Why do I have a feeling it had to do with that note you got?''

''How did you know?''

''A lucky guess.''

She told him about the nightmare—and the disturbing news report she'd watched. Then she went to the desk. ''I got another message.'' Picking up the folded piece of paper, she took it over to Todd.

With sober concentration, he studied the communication. ''Have you considered going to the police?''

''No,'' she responded quickly. ''What could they do?''

Todd shrugged, though the worry in his eyes was plain enough. ''I'm not sure.'' He indicated the piece of paper in his hands. ''One thing is certain, Rachel. We're dealing with someone who's not playing with a full deck.''

Her mouth curved up slightly. ''Or as Meg put it, someone who doesn't have all his oars in the water.''

"You told Meg about the notes?"

"Yes." Rachel briefly related last evening to him, how she and Meg had spent hours searching the *Windjammer* for suspects. Without considering the consequences, she retrieved Meg's list and gave it to Todd.

"Jeff Martin. Sidney Wetherly." Todd read the names aloud. "Sue Peters." He gave Rachel an astonished look that made her promptly wish she could snatch the list back. "Kerrie Bowles." On that one, he merely frowned at her.

"Only Jeff is a suspect as far as I'm concerned," she hastened to assure him.

"Maybe you shouldn't jump to conclusions."

Todd's reply wasn't what she expected, but his next question was. "But why *Sue?*"

That was the tough one, she had to admit. Rachel bit her lip, searching for a diplomatic answer. She couldn't come up with one. "Sue was Meg's idea," she began cautiously. "It shocked me too, and I don't for one second believe Sue would do such a thing as . . . as this." Rachel indicated the ominous message. "But the truth is that. . . . " She hesitated again.

"Go on," Todd coaxed, leaning close to her.

"The truth is, Sue's had a crush on you for years." Todd's startled expression caused Rachel to stop. She was grateful she hadn't told him that the more accurate description of Sue's feelings toward him would be "love."

"I had no clue, Rachel. Honestly."

How could she doubt him when he looked so genuinely distressed? She touched his chin. "I know that."

"Is that why you asked me to dance with Sue? You were trying to steer me in her direction?"

"Only at first. And even then, it would have been a terrible sacrifice."

The confession brought a small smile to Todd's face.

"I'm sorry, Rachel. Maybe I should have recognized the signs, but when I danced with Sue, I didn't see . . . I didn't detect anything there."

"You didn't notice how attracted she is to you?"

"Frankly, no."

That puzzled Rachel, but she was eager to seize the opportunity to switch the focus of their conversation. "Well, like I said, I'm sure Jeff's the perpetrator. It has to be him."

"What about Sidney? Didn't he have a thing for you in school?"

"You knew about that?" She probably shouldn't be surprised.

Todd's mouth curved in a hint of a smile. "Didn't just about everyone?" He grew serious again. "There's something a little off about Sidney. I agree with Meg. You shouldn't rule him out."

At least Rachel could take comfort in the fact that Todd and Meg were in agreement again.

"And then there's Kerrie," he added.

Rachel wondered what to reply. She'd already said too much about Sue. "I would hardly think it's Kerrie either," she replied carefully.

"Why not?" Todd shifted, averting his eyes for a moment. "Rachel, I hate to tell you this, but . . ." His gaze came back to hers. "While I was in Chicago, Kerrie left a message on my answering machine."

Rachel automatically stiffened. "She did?"

"Basically, the reason she called was to ask me to accompany her to a fashion industry dinner next week." His hands came up to rest on Rachel's shoulders.

She tried to smile. "Will you accept?" she asked as playfully as the tightness in her throat would allow.

Todd's fingers gripped her arms almost painfully. "You should know better," he replied in a gruff tone. "Of course not."

"I'm sorry, Todd. I had no right to ask that."

His expression softened. "You had every right. Besides, I've met Kerrie's type before, and she doesn't interest me. Your type does." He slid his fingers lightly down the curve of her hair, stopping at her chin. Then, without warning, he rose from the sofa.

Extending his hand to Rachel, he helped her to her feet. "I've got to stop by the office this morning and you have to be at the store soon." He said it reluctantly.

This time his arm came around her waist, holding her close as they walked to the door. "Would you like to come home first this evening or should I pick you up at Cabbage Rose's?"

"I can take the bus instead of driving to the store and you can pick me up there, if it's convenient for you." She could take a change of clothes with her.

"Very convenient." He stopped in the doorway, looking down at her. "How about six-thirty?"

"Wonderful, Todd." As she watched him go, Rachel determined that she wouldn't allow disquieting thoughts about any would-be stalker to intrude on the happiness she felt at that moment. There were too many positive things happening in her life. Like dinner with Todd's family, for one.

Chapter Seven

It was five-thirty the next afternoon when Rachel decided to close the boutique early. The half hour or so before Todd arrived would give her time to dash to the newsstand for a paper as well as change her clothes.

Business had been brisk all day and, though she was tired, Rachel was glad the hours had passed quickly. Not only had the money taken in been good for the financial health of her shop, but the bustle of customers had been good for her mental health as well. It had kept her mind occupied so that she hadn't been prone to dwell on sinister thoughts.

She posted the CLOSED sign and hurried to change outfits before jostling her way to the newsstand a few doors down from Cabbage Rose's. At the stand, she picked up a copy of the evening paper and handed the money to Sammy, the middle-aged proprietor.

"Hi, gorgeous," he said to her with a wink.

Rachel smiled. "How's it going, Sammy?"

Sammy shrugged, scratching his bald head. "Not so bad. Yourself?"

"Great, just great." Her already good mood heightened by the friendly exchange, Rachel scanned the magazine rack and selected the latest issue of a fashion journal. She was about to pay for it when she felt an odd prickle at the back of her neck. It was the same eerie sensation she'd had that night at Nunzio's when she'd caught someone staring at her.

She tensed automatically, her high spirits plunging. She was barely able to look around her in the crush of people pressing in to buy magazines and newspapers, but she didn't see any familiar faces. "Just nerves," she muttered to herself.

She set her eyes on the magazine in her hand; the words and pictures seemed distorted. Anxiously glancing around a second time, she finally saw what it was that caused her discomfort. And the sight made her freeze in place, the warm blood in her veins turning ice cold.

Jeff Martin was standing only yards away from her. He was almost concealed by the milling crowd, but one thing wasn't hidden from her—his eyes. They were glued on her, his face a mask of intense concentration.

His words—they surely must be his—ran through her mind like a litany. *"You can't get away from me, Rachel. This is a warning! Be careful!"*

Rachel let out a cry and fairly threw the magazine onto the counter in front of her. Dimly, she heard Sammy call, "Hey, Rachel! Are you okay?" as she fled.

It wasn't until she reached the shop, unlocked the door, and was safely inside that she realized what a spectacle she must have been to the other customers at the newsstand. She scolded herself for behaving that way.

Expelling a long breath, she sagged against the door frame for a moment. Everything had happened so quickly; there'd been no chance to think. It *was* Jeff she had seen, wasn't it? Or had her eyes been playing tricks on her? Perhaps it hadn't been Jeff after all, only a man who bore an uncanny resemblance to him.

"No!" Rachel shook the idea from her head. She knew she hadn't been mistaken. Moving away from the door, she had just enough presence of mind to check the time. It was nearly six. She had mere minutes to pull herself together before Todd came for her.

Praying he wouldn't be early, Rachel rushed to the washroom and surveyed her image in the mirror over the sink. The only visible signs that she was upset were the slight pallor in her cheeks, the tiny tremor in her lower lip. It helped that the beige pantsuit she wore was particularly flattering. It had come into the shop the day before and happened to be her size. And the necklace Todd had given her was the perfect complement to the suit.

But the fit of her suit was small consolation for the shakiness that gripped her. Reaching for the bottle of aspirin, she took two with a glass of water to ward off the throbbing at her temples. Then she faced the mirror again.

"You will not allow Jeff Martin to spoil your evening, nor your life," Rachel told herself sternly. At that instant, there was a knock at the outside door. It had to be Todd. Lifting her chin a notch, she put on her best smile and hoped, just this once, that he wouldn't discern her mood.

Rachel followed Todd's mother, Carolyn, into the kitchen. Both of them carried a stack of plates and saucers.

"These are very lovely dishes," Rachel remarked as she joined Carolyn at the counter by the sink. "Todd told me that they originally belonged to his great-grandmother."

"That's right." Carolyn picked up one of the plates from the stack she'd put on the counter. She tapped the finely embellished rim. "Did he also by chance mention that I only use them on very special occasions?" She gave Rachel a smile.

For the first time since she'd arrived, Rachel felt a twinge of self-consciousness in Carolyn Andrews' presence. "Yes." Turning away for an instant to set her stack aside, she offered, "I'll help you load the dishwasher."

"That won't be necessary. Just pile them in the sink." At Rachel's questioning glance, Carolyn added, "Todd does the washing up around here when he's home. He says it's in his blood."

Rachel began to understand. "He told me about that too."

Carolyn laughed and Rachel was able to relax again. The evening had gone well—even better than she'd expected. There'd been almost no awkwardness between herself and Mr. and Mrs. Andrews, as if it had been just yesterday she'd last seen them instead of years ago. That struck her as both extremely satisfying and slightly discomforting, though she couldn't say why.

She'd recalled that Robert Andrews was a quiet man, but tonight he'd been more talkative, showing special interest in her boutique. And Carolyn had been extremely gracious. It was apparent she'd gone all out to put her guest at ease.

"The berry cobbler was delicious," Rachel told her hostess. "I'd love to have your recipe."

Carolyn appeared pleased. "I'll write it down for you before you leave." She started to say something else when Todd came into the kitchen.

He rubbed his hands together. "I can't wait to get started." His eyes were on Rachel and, if she'd dared, she might have asked him if it was merely the idea of the task ahead that made him so eager.

"Here." His mother threw him an apron she'd plucked from a drawer. Then she handed one to Rachel. "Usually he does them alone," Carolyn remarked casually.

"But tonight I feel the need for an assistant," Todd added. "Would you be willing to volunteer, Rachel?"

"Oh, I might consider the idea," she teased, realizing that the prospect of washing stacks of plates and saucers had never been so appealing before.

Carolyn cleared her throat. "Well, since it looks like you two will be occupied here for a while, I'm going to go prop my feet up somewhere and copy that recipe. I believe I've got a couple of others in my file that you'd enjoy trying too, Rachel." She started for the door.

Rachel called after her, "Thanks, Carolyn. My file could use a little help."

When they were alone, Todd held his apron out for inspection. "Ah, no ruffles," he said as he began to loop it over his head. "Promise not to laugh."

Rachel raised her hand. "I swear." But she was already giggling as she watched him adjust the apron in front, then pull its strings around to his back. "Do you want me to tie it for you?" she asked lightly, all the while thinking how utterly manly he looked despite the frock.

"Too late! It's all done," he replied with a sweep of his hand, turning so she could see that he'd made a perfect, if large, bow out of the strings. "But let me help you." He advanced on her before she had time to respond.

He took the apron from her hands and fitted the top over her head, lifting her hair so that it didn't catch in the loop. His arms came to circle her waist; he tied the apron's strings. When he finished, he kept her in his embrace. "Are you having a good time, Rachel?"

She was sure he knew her answer before she gave it. "Wonderful." That drew a pleased grin from him. Rachel had to smile too. She'd obviously managed to hide her earlier upset from him. And in the cozy environment of his parents' home, it wasn't difficult for her to distance any ominous ideas about her frightening encounter with Jeff.

Between Todd and his parents there was an atmosphere of affection and respect that Rachel felt very much at ease with, even if it caused her to feel a certain lonely ache. Too many months had passed since she'd last visited her own family.

"What are you thinking?" Todd whispered, regarding her with interest.

Rachel shrugged. "Just that San Francisco seems awfully far away from St. Paul."

"You miss your folks. I missed mine too when I was in Seattle. But that's what airplanes are for, Rachel."

She smiled up at him. "Yes. I'm planning a trip out to see Mom and Dad in September."

"Good." He looked happy for her. "Now. . . . " He released her and turned on the faucet, running water into one half of the double sink. Steam rose through the air. "This is the fun part." He finished with a wave of his hand.

Yes, the chore was definitely going to be fun, she decided as she watched Todd dump a capful of detergent into the water.

"Wash or dry?" he asked as he stirred the water. Soon bubbles frothed up, nearly overflowing the sink.

"Dry," she chose.

Todd put the serving dishes and plates into the soapy brew and filled the other side of the sink with plain hot water. All the while he whistled a snappy tune that Rachel couldn't quite identify.

"You really are into doing dishes, aren't you?"

"Even more so tonight," he retorted. Submerging his hands in the water, he brought up a plate and gently scrubbed it clean. "Have to be careful, though, with Mom's good china." He slipped the plate into the rinse water. "Drying towels are in the top drawer to your left."

Rachel plucked a towel from the drawer and lifted the plate out of the water to dry it. She hoped she didn't make a klutz out of herself by dropping a piece of the china.

Todd continued his tune as he washed the plates and placed them in her side of the sink. "Are you sure you wouldn't rather be employed by Nunzio's than Silverthorne?" she said. "Or, do you find yourself whistling at work too?"

He stopped his little concert. "Occasionally, but I have to admit the idea of scrubbing pots and pans at Nunzio's holds a certain attraction. That is, if free pizza and spaghetti are part of the wages." He grinned.

Rachel grinned back. "Tell me about your meeting in Chicago. Tell me more about your position with Silverthorne." She could see the request pleased him, but was she all that eager to know?

"There's not a whole lot to tell," he began, thoroughly washing the inside of the bowl that had held the mashed potatoes at dinner. "I did pick up some helpful pointers in Chicago on the development of various types of projects, everything from condo complexes to shopping malls to resorts by the lake. That last one might be a reality for Silverthorne by next summer."

"A new resort on Lake Superior?"

Todd shook his head. "It's going to be fantastic, Rachel, according to Bradley."

Todd's exuberance left Rachel feeling unsettled. If only he weren't so impressed with his boss. She took her time drying the serving bowl. Finally, she said, "And what about the Atrium project?"

"We're in the final phase of negotiations on that right now. Only a few more hurdles to clear with the city and we should be ready to break ground in the fall."

Rachel wondered if clearing those hurdles involved under-the-table deals that Todd wasn't aware of. Forcing a bright smile, she replied, "I'd say that's pretty exciting news. It sounds like Silverthorne is a company on the move."

"Definitely on the move," Todd confirmed. Wiping his hands on his apron, he turned to her and gently grasped her shoulders. "I have something else to tell you, Rachel." He paused, looking away for a second. Then his gaze met hers, unwavering. "Today, at the office, Bradley pulled me aside. He caught me by surprise, but what he had to say amazed me even more."

Rachel's eyes widened with curiosity. "What was that?"

"He said he was near to completing a proposal for me, a project I should be able to start work on by winter."

"Your own project?"

"Yes." His face wore an expression of triumph.

"Oh, Todd." She gave him a hug. Despite any apprehensions she might have about Silverthorne, she knew Todd was genuinely enthused about his job. But her own joy over his advancement was tempered once more by Meg's warning about the company. Leaning back from him, she asked, "Did Bradley mention what the project will be?"

"No, but I should learn soon. It'll be a great opportunity for me, Rachel. I can't tell you how it makes me feel for Bradley Silverthorne to have that kind of confidence in me."

"I understand," she replied, averting her eyes briefly.

"Hey, are you all right?" he asked, holding her just a little tighter.

He must think she was given to moods. "I'm fine," she protested with a smile.

They regarded each other for another moment before he released her and went back to washing dishes. At the bottom of the stack was the huge platter that earlier had been piled high with pork chops. After washing it, Todd dipped the platter in the rinse water, then held it up so that it caught the light.

Leaning close to Rachel, he said, "Look."

She did, and saw their faces partially reflected in the shiny, oval plate.

"My parents have a very happy marriage," he told her as they gazed at each other in the mirrored surface. "A relationship built on respect for each other." He paused. "To me, these dishes symbolize the enduring love between Mom and Dad."

"That's beautiful," Rachel whispered. There was something beautiful as well in the soft, fuzzy appearance of their faces so close together.

"I'm glad you think so." He lowered the platter and placed it in her hands.

Slowly, she dried it, sensing his eyes were on her.

"Rachel . . ."

"Yes?"

"I love my job, but the reason for my happiness lately isn't tied up with work."

She raised her eyes to meet his, anticipating his next words, yet wishing she wasn't impatient to hear them.

"My happiness has everything to do with you, Rachel. Everything," he emphasized.

Her composure was threatened by the intensity of his

words. With caution, she laid the platter down on the counter, using the task as an excuse to escape Todd's gaze. Why couldn't she voice her own feelings toward him? Did he wonder at her silence too?

When she finally looked up, Rachel saw doubt dim the excitement in his eyes. Then it vanished as he reached out to take her hand in his.

"Tell me you'll see me tomorrow, Rachel."

"I'll see you tomorrow." No promise had ever been simpler to make.

Todd gave a short, almost nervous, laugh. "I know things are happening awfully fast between us." She nodded in response. "But I can't help it. I feel like it's been forever."

She thought of his prior confession that he had fallen in love with her at fifteen. "I—" she began haltingly. "I care for you a lot, Todd." An understatement if she'd ever uttered one. "It's just that I want to be sure this is right for us . . . for me."

"I understand," he assured her quietly. "But remember, my heart's known the truth for a very long time." He cupped her hand in his and brought it to his lips. "I don't want to rush you. I want you to be as certain about us as I am."

At that moment, there was a discreet knock at the kitchen door. After the slightest pause, Todd called out, "Come in, Mom." He kept hold of Rachel's hand as his mother bustled into the kitchen.

"Almost done?" Carolyn asked.

"Just the silverware and a few pots," her son replied.

"I thought we could have coffee in the den. I've dug out some photos I thought Rachel might enjoy looking at."

Rachel glanced at Todd. He rolled his eyes. "Don't tell me you've found those ones Dad took at the lake way back when." He grimaced, directing his next comment at Rachel. "I was twelve and about five feet tall with bird legs."

Rachel knew from earlier appraisals of his jeans-clad physique that there were no bird legs there now. Definitely not. "You've just piqued my curiosity, Todd," she murmured. "I'd love to see the photos," she added in response to his mother.

"I'll make the coffee while you two finish the dishes," Carolyn said with a grin identical to her son's.

The weekend passed in a happy blur for Rachel—the evening spent with Todd and his parents, a Sunday afternoon picnic with Todd in Como Park, followed by paddleboating on the park's lake until dusk. Then settling down with him under the gathering stars to listen to a concert by the St. Paul Symphony Orchestra. Finally, quiet conversation and iced coffee in a downtown bistro.

All in all, it had been an idyllic two days, and when Monday morning came, Rachel found it frustratingly difficult to concentrate on the practical matter of running a business.

But if what she needed was a dose of reality to get her feet back on terra firma again, she got it in the unexpected person of Sammy.

He came by the boutique just after she'd opened for the day. He'd never been inside before and his presence there wakened in her the memory of her frantic flight from his newsstand—and its cause.

"Hi, Sammy," she said, mustering a brave smile. "What can I do for you? A dress or blouse for your wife, maybe?" She hoped that was the reason for his visit.

"Hi, Rachel," he returned, ducking his head in a shy way. Though there weren't any customers in the store, he was obviously uncomfortable. "I'm sorry. No dress today," he said apologetically. He cleared his throat; she steeled herself for what he would say next. "This is why I'm here." Sammy thrust a piece of paper toward her.

She took it, both surprised and puzzled. Motioning for him to follow her to the counter, she laid the piece of paper down and looked it over. There were a number of signatures on it; she recognized several as those of other Arcade tenants. "What's this?" she asked.

"A petition." Sammy's mouth tilted up at her questioning glance. Then he grew sober. "You got one of those tenants' surveys in the mail, didn't you?"

"Yes," she replied a bit guiltily, not telling him that she'd forgotten to respond to it.

Sammy nodded. "Well, rumor has it that somebody's trying to make a deal with Mineola. For the Arcade."

"You mean Penny Lane might be changing owners? How do you know that?"

"Got the news from Will."

Will Abrams ran a watch and jewelry repair shop next to Sammy's newsstand. He'd told her once that he'd been a tenant of the Arcade since it opened. "How did Will learn about a possible sale? Did he say who the buyer might be?"

Sammy shrugged. "He doesn't know yet who the buyer is, but you can be sure he'll find out."

Rachel liked Will and no doubt he was as reliable a source as any concerning information about Penny Lane. Still, she was a bit skeptical.

"That isn't all Will heard. That's why we're passing this petition."

Rachel wasn't sure she wanted to hear the rest. "Go on, Sammy."

He clasped his hands together in front of him. "It seems that whoever gets the Arcade is sure to raise rents. Will and I reckon that means most of us'll be forced to relocate . . . or go out of business."

Rachel swallowed hard. Without a doubt, that "most"

included her. She reached for a pen. Before she signed her name to the petition, she carefully read the several lines of print above the signatures. It was an appeal to keep Penny Lane Arcade under its present ownership and management.

"We're sending the original to Miles Preston and a copy to Bob West," explained Sammy as Rachel added her name to the list.

Miles Preston was the president of Mineola Property Company and Bob West was the property manager for the Arcade. "Bob's treated us well, hasn't he?"

"He has," Sammy agreed. "Let's hope that good relationship continues." He took the petition and started for the door. As he was about to exit the shop he looked back at her. A frown etched his ruddy face. "I meant to ask. Is everything okay with you . . . and with the store?"

Rachel's heart missed a beat. "Yes, fine, Sammy," she said a little too fast.

He regarded her thoughtfully. "I was just wondering because the other day at the newsstand you seemed in an awful hurry, like—" He shrugged. "As if you were scared." Giving a short laugh, he added, "The expression on your face made me think you'd seen a ghost or something."

Rachel laughed too; it echoed in her ears like the nervous twitter of a bird. "No ghost, I promise you. It wasn't anything, Sammy, just that I . . . I'd forgotten to lock the shop before I went for the paper." The lie left an unsavory taste in her mouth. She'd always loathed dishonesty in any form. Yet she couldn't bring herself to tell him the real reason she'd fled from the newsstand.

"Oh," was his only reaction. But when he didn't move to leave, she wondered if he saw through her fib. Then suddenly he swung the door back and started out.

"I'll be seeing you, Rachel," he called over his shoulder, "and thanks for your support on the petition."

"No problem. I hope it does some good," she returned. Her eyes followed him the few steps to the card and gift shop next door where he went in.

Leaning against the wall, Rachel closed her eyes as her fingers worked the knot at the base of her neck. The news Sammy had brought about the possible sale of the Arcade wasn't good, though she was grateful that he and Will were trying to do something to help all the tenants of the complex.

But her greater concern at the moment was his remembrance of her sudden flight from his newsstand. If Sammy had noticed her fear, wouldn't Jeff have too? Did it give Jeff a morbid satisfaction to know she was afraid? An image of the Broadway star, Flora Gonzales, flashed in her mind. Purposely, Rachel had avoided the evening newscasts since hearing of the murder. Was it because she didn't want to know that the actress had met death at the hands of a stalker?

Rachel sighed in the silence of the shop. She had an overpowering urge to call Todd, which she immediately cast aside. He had promised to phone her that evening. She told herself she could wait until then. But there was another kind of waiting that seemed interminable. The first two anonymous messages had come on successive Fridays. Today was only Monday. She had four more days to go.

Chapter Eight

When she arrived home that evening, Rachel found two messages on her answering machine. She switched on the machine and heard Todd's voice.

"Hi, Rachel," he began. "Has it been only fourteen hours since we were together? It seems like weeks since I've seen you," he continued, his voice low, its rich texture enhanced somehow by the machine's speaker. A small quiver of pleasure went through Rachel.

"I was hoping to see you this evening, but Bradley called a meeting to discuss the Atrium project. I have to be there, but know that my heart's with you. I'll call tomorrow. Sweet dreams tonight, Rachel."

Rachel felt a stab of disappointment as she switched off the recorder for a moment. Why did she believe she must see Todd or her day wouldn't be complete? She brought herself up short. It was past time to start gaining at least a modicum of control over her emotions, the

116

ones that were kindled whenever she saw Todd—or thought about him.

But what of those other emotions, the bleaker reflections that seemed to be consuming more and more of her attention? It was getting harder to dismiss the uneasy sensation that followed her everywhere like a storm cloud, mutely warning her that Jeff might be concealed behind that last doorway or crouched just ahead in some blind alley, tracking her with his grim, unblinking eyes.

"Stop it!" she reprimanded herself, slamming down on the button that started the tape again. The voice that floated through the air caused Rachel to jump.

"Rachel? Hi, it's Sue." There was a pause and then, "I've got some news. Diane called from New York. She and Derek are coming early and she wondered if we could get together this weekend. I checked with Mickey and we decided on Saturday at noon. We thought we could meet at Anthony's for lunch." Another pause. "I hope you don't mind that we didn't check with you first. Call me if you can't come then and we'll find another time. Otherwise, we'll plan to see you Saturday."

Rachel digested the information with detachment. Normally, her reaction would have been one of anticipation. But at the moment, it was more like dread.

Not sure why, Rachel rewound the tape and played both messages again. Todd's provoked a small smile, but her expression became contemplative as she listened to Sue's call. The usual animation was gone from Sue's voice. Could it be due to fatigue—or wariness? Maybe Sue was also less than enthusiastic about the prospect of having to act chummy with a woman she believed was an obstacle on the path of true love.

Clenching her hands together, she determined that she would get Sue alone for a moment on Saturday and pin her to a date to visit Cabbage Rose's—all on pretext, of course, as Meg had suggested. One thing, though, had changed.

Meg had pronounced her ''noble.'' Rachel wondered what Meg would label her if she knew her friend had no intention of sacrificing her relationship with Todd for Sue's feelings, even though she wished to stay on good terms with Sue.

Todd himself had fueled her determination with his admission that he hadn't any idea Sue cared for him— now or a decade ago. And he'd certainly shown no interest in dating Sue. But Rachel had to acknowledge that his feelings toward her could hardly be misconstrued, whatever her own insecurities about their relationship.

With a sigh, Rachel shut off the answering machine and moved to the kitchen. She was anxious to put the matter concerning Sue out of her mind. As before, she couldn't.

Absently, she took a carton of orange juice from the refrigerator and poured herself a glass. Leaning against the counter, she sipped the beverage. It tasted bitter, not sweet.

Rachel wondered if the juice was turning rancid. Without finishing it, she poured the beverage into the sink and washed it away with water from the tap. If only she could easily dismiss the worries that crowded her head. Helpless to stop herself, she went over the list of them again.

The anonymous messages. Her own implacable certainty that Jeff was the sender, that he was stalking her for whatever devious reasons his mind had conjured up. Her tenuous relationship with Sue. Oh yes, and a vague uneasiness that kept telling her love needn't move at warp speed, that it would be for her own benefit to step back and analyze her relationship with Todd in a logical manner.

And there was yet another concern: Sammy's news about the possible sale of Penny Lane.

Rachel shook her head, wishing the act could remove every distressful thought. She traced her steps back into the living room and went to the double doors that led to her balcony. In the midst of opening them, she suddenly stopped. A picture of Jeff watching her from around the corner of the newsstand seared her mind as she looked down and saw the blackness that marked the area of the park. Might he be there, hidden in the shadows, with a pair of binoculars in his hands trained on her balcony? The very idea was ridiculous.

Yet, with a motion born more of instinct than plan, Rachel slammed the doors shut and pulled the drapes tight until not even the barest trace of night was visible in the place where the curtains came together. Her heart thumped wildly as she leaned against the wall for a moment.

Enough, she scolded herself. But when she tried to go about her normal routine of fixing the usual light dinner and selecting the clothes she wanted to wear the next day, she found herself making any number of foolish blunders. Like leaving the burner on and the potholder lying close enough to be badly singed. Or choosing the very blouse, a pale yellow number with frilly ruffles, that she hadn't worn because she'd hated it from the day after she'd bought it.

In the end, she hadn't done her meal justice, sending most of it down the garbage disposal. And after she realized she'd never wear the blouse, she placed it back on its hanger. She would take the garment with her in the morning and put it on sale at the shop. What was that old adage? One woman's junk is another woman's treasure? A smile briefly lifted the corners of Rachel's mouth.

At least she'd been decisive about something and it

made her feel good. Though the evening was pretty well wasted, there were a couple of reasons to look forward to the next day. One was the hope of at least talking with Todd. The other was that it would be the Tuesday of the month when she went over her account ledger.

Rachel did her account the old-fashioned way, without a computer. She got pleasure from the task, even when the columns didn't show as much profit as she would have liked. And if, in the morning, her mind was filled with debits and credits and due bills, there wouldn't be room for anything else until the job was finished.

By lunchtime Tuesday, Rachel had completed going over the ledger. She was consoled by the final tally that showed Cabbage Rose's had turned a tidy profit for the month. But once the books were closed, a sense of restlessness set in and she began to wish she could talk to Meg.

The Plymouth Building was only a couple of blocks from the Arcade. Without bothering to call first to see if her friend was in, Rachel posted the CLOSED sign in the boutique window and started up the sidewalk.

The afternoon was warm, on the muggy side, yet saved by a light breeze. But Rachel's mind wasn't on the weather. At the imposing glass doors of the Plymouth Building, she paused for an instant, then entered. Marge, the receptionist who sat at the ultramodern mauve desk in the lobby, greeted Rachel with a perfunctory smile.

Rachel walked past the fountain and lush foliage that was the focal point of the lobby, and headed for the elevators. One was open; she stepped inside and pressed the button for the fourth floor. The elevator carried her smoothly upward. A soft ringing sound told her she'd arrived at her floor. It seemed forever before the door slid back. When it did, she hurried toward Meg's office.

"Rach! I can't believe it. I was just thinking of you!" Meg rose from her desk at the sight of her friend in the doorway.

Rachel smiled, glancing around the cramped but neat room. "I guess my feet must have known. They seemed to direct me over here of their own volition."

"Well, I'd say your feet are on the ball," Meg quipped, drawing a laugh from Rachel. "Sit down," she ordered. "Or did you come to ask me to lunch?"

"I'm sorry, Meg. I already ate." It was true, though the meal had consisted of half a tuna sandwich washed down with a few swallows of water. Rachel started to settled herself in the chair beside Meg's desk. "If you have plans, I can come back another—"

Meg cut her off with a wave and a grin. "My plan is to sit right here and eat my dull cheese and crackers." She held up a cellophane-wrapped packet for Rachel's inspection. "But I do have some iced peppermint tea if you'd care for a glass.

"I'd love some."

Meg reached inside the cabinet beside her desk and retrieved a thermos and two paper cups. She poured the beverage into the cups, handing one to Rachel. "It's cold. There's even ice cubes in it."

Rachel inspected her tea. "I see." She took a careful sip. "It's good, Meg."

Meg smiled, but her eyes were serious. "You didn't drop by just for tea, Rach."

"No." Rachel cradled the cup in her hands.

"What is it?" Meg leaned forward on her elbows. "You got another anonymous message?" she guessed. When Rachel didn't reply, she went on, "You and Todd had an argument."

Rachel held up her hand. "No, not that." She regarded Meg. "In fact, Todd and I are so happy that it kind of . . . scares me." Meg's reaction was no reaction.

Drinking another swallow of tea, Rachel took note of a photograph of Phil that sat on a shelf beside Meg's desk. He was smiling, his eyes crinkling merrily behind wire-rimmed glasses. "Have you and Phil set the date yet?"

That drew a short laugh from Meg. "No, but we're close. You didn't come here to discuss my wedding plans either."

Rachel's eyes went unfocused for a moment. "I guess I didn't." Glancing back at Meg, she said, "I'm going to see Sue on Saturday. She, Diane, Mickey, and I are having lunch together."

"And you'll get Sue alone?"

"I'm taking your suggestion." That seemed to meet with Meg's approval. "You might be interested to know that Kerrie Bowles called Todd and asked him for a date."

Meg's eyebrows went up. "He didn't accept, of course."

Rachel shook her head. "Uh-uh. But I have a feeling she won't give up."

"Probably not," was Meg's only comment.

Rachel went on to relate her encounter with Jeff at the newsstand. There was a sense of relief in being able to tell Meg about it.

"You're more convinced than ever that Jeff's the stalker, aren't you?"

Returning Meg's level gaze, Rachel replied, "I am. It's like I've started to look for him everywhere now." Her voice almost a whisper, she added, "I don't want him to take over my life again."

"Then you haven't seen Sidney around?"

So Meg still entertained the notion that Sidney could be the stalker. "No, I haven't."

Meg picked up a pen and tapped it against the desk.

"But Kerrie obviously hasn't given up on Todd. And we can't be sure about Sue, can we?"

"Todd wants me to go to the police," she countered.

"Why haven't you?" Meg responded swiftly.

"What could they do? Jeff . . . I mean, the stalker hasn't actually threatened me. They'll probably think I'm foolish, that I should consider the notes just a sick joke." She paused. "That's what I believed . . . at first."

"I agree with Todd. You should go to the authorities, Rach. Promise me you will if you get any more notes, or if you see *anyone* looking at you in a way that makes you uncomfortable."

"In other words, any person, male or female, who glances at me cross-eyed."

The remark died on the air and Rachel sought to change the topic of conversation to a subject only a bit less disturbing. She related Sammy's news about the impending sale of Penny Lane.

Meg grabbed a square of blank paper from a notepad on her desk. She jotted something on it. "I should be able to find out in a jiffy whether Sammy's story is true. I'll get Jason to check it out. He's one of our top salesmen," she revealed. "Young and very ambitious, like Todd."

Rachel hoped it was a compliment to both men. "Thanks. I really appreciate it." She finished her tea.

Meg rose and came around the desk. She gave Rachel a hug. "That's what friends are for. Right?"

"Right.

Let me take you to lunch next week, Meg," she said on impulse.

"Okay, but only if you promise me you'll go to the police the moment the stalker contacts you again."

"All right. I promise." Rachel held up her hands, hoping the hastily spoken words would appease Meg. "For now, I'd better get back to the store."

"I'll walk with you as far as the lobby," Meg offered, motioning for Rachel to follow her. On the way to the elevator, they consulted their pocket calendars and decided to have lunch together the next Wednesday.

"I should have some news for you by then," Meg said as they lingered for a moment near Marge's desk. "I know that I'd be anxious to find out whether my means of livelihood was about to be sold out from under me."

Emotion rose in Rachel's throat, almost blocking her words. "Since you put it that way, I admit I am." She turned from Meg and headed resolutely in the direction of the place that was very much her "means of livelihood."

It was the middle of what had turned into a slow afternoon when Rachel heard someone enter the shop. Peering up to see who it was, her surprise was soon supplanted by delight. "I can't believe you're here!" She couldn't hide the excitement in her voice.

Todd stood just inside the door, a wide smile on his face. "I happened to be in the neighborhood again. Are you busy?" A glance around the shop could have told him she wasn't.

But his gaze never shifted from her as he made fast work of the distance between them. He bent to kiss her before she could respond. When he drew back, he said, "You'll go out to dinner with me tonight, won't you?"

Even if she'd had plans, could she have said no? Securely captured in his embrace, she declared, "You're spoiling me."

"If that's what I'm doing, I'm having a wonderful time of it." Though she hadn't quite said yes, he went on, "As usual, I'll be by for you after closing?"

Rachel whispered, "All right, Todd," and he released

her. She braced herself against the wall, smiling, while he exited the shop as swiftly as he'd entered.

Todd Andrews appeared to be very much a man of impulse. She decided it had to be one of the things that made him unbearably attractive to her. Not to mention the air of self-assurance that he projected—never a sense of cockiness, but a quiet determination that told her with every look, every touch, he was out to win her and would accept nothing less than victory. And even if she couldn't say so aloud for fear it was too glorious to be true, the idea was becoming more and more agreeable to her.

"You're quiet tonight." Rachel peered expectantly at Todd across the banquette table. As exuberant as he'd been that afternoon, his mood over dinner had seemed more one of contemplation. They had talked, laughed even, but their conversation had centered mainly on the meal they'd ordered and the ambience of the small French café where neither had dined before.

Now Todd returned her gaze as his hand reached to claim hers. "I'm sorry if I'm not very good company."

"You're always good company," she promptly rejoined.

He smiled. "I'm glad you think so." His eyes left hers to travel over the smartly appointed room where they were seated. "We'll have to come back here."

"Yes, we will. The food's delicious." Rachel sensed he had something on his mind. She hadn't broached any of the subjects she'd discussed with Meg at lunch, not wanting to put a damper on their evening together. Did he suspect she was hiding her worries from him? Or was he preoccupied with concerns of his own? "Todd, is anything the matter?"

His fingers caressed hers. "No," he said, not very convincingly.

"Kerrie didn't call you again by chance?" she inquired in a softly cajoling tone. As soon as the question was out of her mouth, Rachel regretted it.

Todd gave her an odd look that made her even more uneasy. "Funny you should ask that." A frown drew the corners of his mouth down. "Kerrie didn't call. She came by my office in person this afternoon."

Rachel let out a small gasp before she could stop herself. Should she be surprised? "I assume she came to ask you for another date," she said, hardly teasing this time.

Todd appeared thoughtful for a moment. "Not exactly. Her mission was to persuade me to try out for a modeling job."

Another gasp rose in Rachel's throat; this time she managed to keep it from escaping. It wasn't shock over the idea that Kerrie would consider Todd model material. And there was no doubt in Rachel's mind that Kerrie would stoop to considerable lengths to snare him. "Are you tempted? I mean I'm sure you could . . . be a model if you wanted to." She hated the way she stumbled over her words.

He gave a short laugh. "The idea might be tempting in certain circumstances." Leaning toward Rachel, he continued, "She came to me uninvited. If I'd been warned, I would've found a reason to be very busy just then."

His response was comforting, but tenacious curiosity caused her to ask, "Did Kerrie give you any particulars, like what kind of modeling you'd be doing, or where?"

"Yes. Modeling swimwear in Acapulco." He seemed to gauge her reaction before adding, "Kerrie claimed her agency is scouting for a few male models for that shoot."

"And naturally, she would think of you." Rachel congratulated herself for the calm way she spoke—while inside she was roiling with anger toward Kerrie.

"Apparently so." Todd hesitated. "I found out that she can be very persuasive when she wants to be."

"I don't doubt that." Rachel forced a smile. "It sounds like an exciting opportunity, Todd." Why was she encouraging him?

"Maybe." Todd let go of her hand. His fingers touched the necklace that was his gift to her. She'd worn it almost every day since that evening. "Remember what I told you before when she asked me out?" He waited for Rachel's acknowledgment. "Well, neither Kerrie nor the idea of a modeling career means anything to me."

His emphatic declaration rumbled through Rachel like a minor earthquake, dispelling the anger. And the way he was regarding her, she was sure he would kiss her if they were alone. Still, she pressed on. "Kerrie wants you, Todd. I don't think she'll give up easily."

"She can't have me because I belong to you."

His words were so hushed, Rachel could have missed them. But she didn't. What he'd said thrilled her, and she yearned to make a reply in kind. Yet it suddenly became impossible to voice the simple truth that she belonged to him too.

The silence between them stretched out; she sensed Todd expected her to say something. She swallowed hard. Unless she soon came to terms with her love for him, wouldn't she be abetting Kerrie's cause? The idea was abhorrent to her.

As if he'd read her thoughts, Todd's face took on a troubled look. But when he spoke, Rachel realized his mind had assumed a different bent. "The messages you've been getting in the mail. . . . " He glanced away, then back at her. "Rachel, I believe you should seriously consider Kerrie as a suspect."

Her reaction was one of immediate skepticism and she couldn't hide it from Todd. For despite her shameless overtures toward him, Kerrie didn't match Rachel's image of the type of person who would resort to sending bizzare messages through the mail. Maybe it was because she was so beautiful, or maybe because she didn't strike Rachel as being that desperate. On the other hand, Rachel knew for a fact that Jeff Martin could be plenty obsessive. And wasn't Sidney Wetherly the epitome of a disturbed personality?

"Rachel?"

Todd's soft inquiry brought Rachel out of her introspection. "I'm sorry. I just can't accept that Kerrie would sit and pen anonymous notes."

"She might, if she thinks you'll become so afraid someone is stalking you that you'll—"

"That my fear will come between us," Rachel conjectured. "Or that our relationship will suffer to the point that we'll break up. And she'll be there to save you, like some perversely feminine knight in tarnished armor."

Neither spoke for several moments. Finally he asked if she would like dessert. When she declined, Todd suggested that they leave.

At his car, before opening the door on her side, he pulled Rachel into his arms and gave her the kiss she knew he'd longed to give her earlier. As they clung to each other, she found herself pouring out her fears to him, revealing her encounter with Jeff and her dread of finding another message in her mailbox on Friday.

"Then I'll be with you on Friday," he whispered against her cheek. "And if there's another message, we're going directly to the nearest police precinct."

It was impossible to argue with him. His arm supported her until she was settled in the front seat of the Prelude. She felt his hand brush a stray wisp of hair from her face. "I love you," he said. Then he shut the door between them and went around to the driver's side.

'I'm sorry, Miss Anders, but even with the new stalking law on the books I'm afraid there isn't much we can do. You see—Lt. Savage indicated the pieces of paper spread out on his desk—"even though you believe your former fiancé sent you these, you admit there's no concrete evidence linking him to the notes." He paused. "Other than your claim that on several occasions you saw him allegedly watching you. . . . " The lieutenant shook his head.

"He *was* watching her," Todd put in emphatically.

Rachel looked at him, then at Lt. Savage. The officer seemed far away somehow, seated as he was opposite them at his massive, cluttered desk.

The lieutenant's mouth twitched a little on one side. "Watching someone in a public place is hardly a crime, Mr. Andrews." He gave a small shrug before directing his attention back to Rachel. "But if you could give me his name, Miss Anders, it would be a start."

Rachel licked her lips. She thought she'd come fully prepared to cooperate with the authorities, to tell them honestly what her suspicions were and why. To tell them too just who it was she believed was menacing her.

But now, with the lieutenant and Todd both staring at her expectantly, the words she needed to say wouldn't come. She opened her mouth, tried to force out Jeff's name—and couldn't. What came out instead was a stammered, "I'm sorry, Lt. Savage, I . . . can't tell you." Rachel bowed her head.

"I can."

Her head jerked up at the determined sound of Todd's voice. "No," she said, eyes meeting his in a silent plea. "You said yourself I can't be sure."

Todd looked at her as though he believed she'd taken

leave of her senses. Turning away from her, his jaw clamped tight. Whether the reaction was one of sheer anger or dismay, she didn't know.

"Well, Miss Anders," the lieutenant's voice began, bringing her attention back to him, "you don't sound very certain of yourself." He shook his head. "It seems what we've established is that no overt threat has been made."

Todd spoke up then. "You don't consider this a threat?" he asked testily, reaching over to lay a finger on the stalker's latest—and most ominous—communication. It had arrived, like the others, in Friday's mail.

The police officer regarded Todd, then Rachel. Was his expression the least condescending? Rachel felt foolish. She wished Todd hadn't insisted that she come here, even though she'd quickly assented.

Finally, Lt. Savage spoke. "It's disturbing, of course." He picked up the note Todd's finger rested on and began to read it aloud. *"Wishing me like to one more rich in hope, featured like him, like him with friends possessed."*

"You say this is Shakespeare and that the notes started coming after you attended your tenth high school reunion?" The lieutenant addressed the question to Rachel. After her affirmative answer, he read on, *"You had everything, Rachel, but you wanted HIM. Now I'm your shadow, the darkness that haunts you. Remember this: I'M WATCHING YOU, I'M WATCHING, WAITING. . . ."*

Rachel trembled; she shut her eyes. *"I'm your shadow, the darkness that haunts you. . . . "* Her eyes opened to find Lt. Savage staring at her.

"I can appreciate your concern, Miss Anders." He appeared somber. "But, like I started to say, until we've got something more concrete to go on, there's not much we can do. I'm sorry." He folded his hands together and leaned back in his chair.

Rachel knew she'd just been dismissed. She glanced at Todd. His face wore a stony expression, his eyes fixed on the lieutenant. His mouth opened as if he were going to say something; then it shut again in a grim line.

Rachel squared her shoulders. "I want to thank you for your time, Lt. Savage." She fought to keep her voice cool and even. "I do understand your position." She started to rise from her chair; the lieutenant followed. At first, Todd didn't move, but after a minute, he too got up.

The lieutenant walked with them to the door of the precinct's headquarters. Rachel turned to go. The officer stopped her briefly with his departing words. "If there are any new developments, Miss Anders, feel free to contact me." His lips curved in a small smile. "We are here to be of help, you know."

It was the first hopeful thing he'd said. Rachel looked at the officer. "I'll do that, Lt. Savage. Thank you again." As she walked away from him, she wondered how he would feel if he knew her chief suspect was a man he most likely had a passing acquaintance with, at least a man who worked in close collaboration with the law. Was that the reason why she'd all at once lost her nerve and kept silent about Jeff?

Outside the precinct building Rachel thought the sun shone with excessive brightness. Her eyes began to water. As she dabbed at them, she told herself the trickle of tears was due to the harsh light.

Neither she nor Todd spoke until they came to his car in the precinct's lot. Once they were both settled inside the vehicle, he turned to her. "Why, Rachel?" His hands gripped her arms. "Why wouldn't you tell him?"

She avoided his eyes, but felt the intensity of his gaze. "I'm a coward. But then, as the lieutenant said, there wasn't anything he could do anyway." Her voice held a sarcastic tone.

"Whatever information you could give him could be

of help,'' Todd countered adamantly. His hold on her loosened. His hands slid up to her shoulders, cupping them. "I just want to understand," he said softly.

At last she raised her eyes. "I'm sorry, Todd. Truly, I am. But I can't answer that myself. Maybe . . . maybe there is a real doubt in my mind that it's Jeff, and I didn't want to implicate an innocent person."

They regarded each other uneasily. Then without a clue as to where the inspiration came from, Rachel said, "I'm going to confront him. I'm going to force Jeff to tell me whether he sent the messages." How she would do this she had no idea.

Todd's swift reaction startled her. "Let's go then." He turned from her to insert the key into the ignition.

Her hand clamped down on his arm. "No, Todd, not *us. Me.*"

The air took on a different sort of electricity as he absorbed what she'd said. He looked at her, his face hardened in an expression of defiance. Those gorgeous eyes glowered at her. "You're crazy if you think I'll let you face Martin alone."

Rachel retreated as far from him as the cramped quarters of the Prelude would allow. But she held his gaze, just as determined as he not to back down. "You don't own me, Todd Andrews," she snapped, "and you're not going to tell me what I can or can't do."

Todd flinched noticeably, and she suddenly wished she could snatch back the heated declaration. Yet, it was true. How many times had she told herself she shouldn't be rushing headlong into this relationship, that she ought to sensibly examine her feelings for Todd?

"You're right, Rachel," he said finally. "I don't own you." His eyes narrowed and his face reddened. She had never seen him so upset before, yet he spoke with an icy calmness. "I'm beginning to wonder if there's someone else who owns you. Jeff Martin, to be specific."

Rachel stared at him, incredulous. "What? How could you even consider such an absurd notion . . . that . . . " she spluttered. "That you would have the nerve to imply I could still care for Jeff after what he did to me!"

"Then tell me again. Why did you withhold his name from Lt. Savage?" Todd's voice rose on the question and he turned away briefly when she didn't respond.

He sighed. After what seemed an eternity, he looked back at her. "You know, you're sending some pretty mixed signals, Rachel. One minute you're acting terrified because you're convinced that Jeff is stalking you. The next, you're begging me not to give the good lieutenant your prime suspect's name. It's time you ask yourself a few hard questions. Like, just what does Martin mean to you."

Rachel couldn't believe what she was hearing. And at once she thought she knew exactly what the problem was. "Todd Andrews, you're jealous." The statement had a certain triumphant ring to it that she savored in her vexed state.

Unexpectedly, Todd reached out to her. "You don't mean that, Rachel," he said in a tone that sounded more taunting than penitent.

Rachel did mean it and she considered, for the first time, whether Todd and Jeff might be cut from the same cloth. It was unimaginable, but had she been duped by a show of Todd's outward charm while inside he shared Jeff's petty, possessive nature?

Pushing his hand away from her with her own, she pleaded, "Just . . . take me home. You're right. I need time to think."

"If that's what you want." Todd's words were thick with weariness.

It was the last thing in the world she wanted. "Yes, it is," she replied with a terrible coldness.

Chapter Nine

""I said, I'm going to the ladies' lounge. Does any-one want to come too?"

Rachel peered up at Diane, who had spoken. Embar-rassed, she said, "I'm sorry. I'm afraid I was daydream-ing." Actually, it had been more like ruminating, though she had no intention of saying so.

She, Diane, Sue, and Mickey had gathered as planned at Anthony's. But through most of the meal Rachel won-dered if it wouldn't have been better for Sue and Diane to have dined alone. Almost before they'd been seated, Sue had announced she was thinking about moving away from St. Paul. Then immediately she'd begun to ply Di-ane with questions about New York—what it was like to live there, which spas were popular with the Wall Street crowd.

Diane had warmed to the subject to the extent that the topic of the Big Apple had dominated the friends' con-versation through the entire meal.

It wasn't that Rachel was angry about it, exactly, though she did feel left out. Perhaps in one respect she should be grateful because she was hardly up for friendly gossip after the troubling events of the day before. Nor had Mickey shown any inclination for small talk. She'd sat in a sullen state the whole time, barely responding the few times Rachel had tried to engage her in conversation. In fact, Rachel had the notion that Mickey was quite ill at ease, even more so than she'd appeared to be the night of the reunion.

"What do you say, Rachel?"

Rachel's attention was drawn back to Diane with a start. Diane was regarding her expectantly. "Okay, I'll go with you. My legs could use a good stretch."

"I'll pass," Sue said.

"Me too," Mickey announced, folding her hands across her chest as she looked from Diane to Rachel.

As soon as they came through the door of the ladies' room, Diane asked, "Are you still seeing him?"

The tiny lounge at once seemed terribly stuffy to Rachel.

"Todd, I mean," Diane went on.

"I . . . was, Diane."

Diane's cheeks took on a crimson hue. "I've asked the wrong question, haven't I? I'm so sorry."

"No. Don't be sorry." Rachel reached for Diane's hand and squeezed it. "We were dating for a while, until just recently. I'm not sure we'll be seeing each other anymore."

Diane looked pained. "You do love him, don't you?" Rachel kept silent. "Oh, I hope whatever's come between you can be resolved. All through high school I thought the two of you would make the most adorable couple. But you were dating Jeff, and you seemed so serious about him. And Todd was dating Stacey."

Rachel gave her friend a wan smile. She knew that

Diane meant well. Hadn't Meg recently made a similar statement? "I don't know about the adorable part, Diane, but it's a horribly romantic notion," she said in a voice that trembled slightly. Not ready to let go of the subject just yet, but wanting to shift the attention away from herself, Rachel added, "Do you remember how crazy Sue was about Todd in high school? She believed the day dawned and darkened on him."

Diane frowned. "I guess maybe she was. But I have to confess that another of my strange notions was that Mickey had a wild crush on Todd too."

Rachel wasn't sure why, but a giggle escaped her mouth. It must have been a release of the tension that had been building all day. "Why would you ever think Mickey had a crush on him?"

Shrugging, Diane replied, "I suspected it in high school, but I was positive I'd been right when I saw Mickey's reaction to Todd at the reunion."

"What kind of reaction?" Rachel was genuinely curious.

"For one, when Todd asked you to dance, she seemed horribly disappointed. And when you and he came to tell us you were leaving early, Mickey looked about as anguished as I was happy." Diane's brow furrowed. "I could be wrong. After all, I haven't seen Mickey or Sue in quite a while. Thinking back, I remember Mickey acted out of sorts all evening, even before Todd crashed our little group."

"I noticed it too. But I believe her mood that night had a lot more to do with Rob Ransom than Todd Andrews." Just to say Todd's name like that caused an ache in Rachel's breast. Then it passed.

"Mickey's awfully quiet today," Diane observed.

"Yes, she is." Rachel remembered another of Meg's insightful comments. For what it was worth, she said, "I wonder if Mickey isn't having a hard time dealing with her new image after being an object of ridicule for so many years.''

"I never considered that, but it could be the case."

"I wish there was some way we could help her."

"That's you, Rachel. Always has been. Even when you're chin deep in trials of your own, you still want to heal everyone else's wounds."

"Someone once said I was noble."

Diane gave her a warm hug. "That someone was right."

When they got back to the table, Diane announced that she hated to break up the party, but she had to meet Derek in half an hour. Then Mickey declared she had to be on her way too, that she had a load of errands to run. Rachel surmised it was pretense on Mickey's part.

Turning to give Mickey a hug, Rachel froze. Across the room was a man. Not just any man. A man whose gaze sent a cold tremor up her spine. "No!" she cried, unable to hide her emotion.

"What is it?"

"What's wrong, Rachel?"

"Are you okay?"

Sue, Diane, and Mickey all clamored to learn what had happened to her so suddenly. She couldn't reply, only lower her hands. After a moment, she told them. "I saw Jeff." With morbid interest she gazed his way again. But he wasn't there.

Had she finally gone off the deep end and just imagined she'd seen him? Furtively, Rachel scanned the room, determined to know the truth. She soon spotted him making a fast course for the exit, his resolute strides carrying him farther away with each step.

Sue's arm came around her. "Rachel, you're shaking. You'd better sit down."

"Don't let him affect you like that. He's a total jerk," Diane put in.

Rachel saw the faces of her three friends, all waiting expectantly. "I can't help it. I've seen him lately in different places. And every time he's . . . been watching me."

"That's creepy," Diane rejoined.

Rachel let out a trembly laugh. "More than creepy. I have reason to suspect he's been stalking me."

"Stalking you?" Mickey spoke up. "Why do you believe he'd do something like that?"

Rachel saw the skepticism etched in her friends' faces along with concern. She couldn't blame them. If it weren't for the evidence, she would consider the idea crazy too. Yet if she were to tell them the whole story, it would mean broaching the subject of Todd. That had been tough enough with just Diane, let alone Sue and Mickey. "Trust me when I say I have my reasons," she said at last.

"You're frightened," Diane chided. "Why can't you tell us? We want to help."

"I know you do." Rachel met Diane's eyes, appealing to her. "I can't say any more just now."

Diane, at least, seemed to sense the topic was closed. "You'll be all right?"

Rachel shook her head, and Diane put her arms around her. "Please be careful, Rachel," she whispered. "Call me any hour, day or night, if you want to talk. I mean it. Promise you will?"

"I promise. Thank you," Rachel whispered back, squeezing her eyes shut against the hot tears that threatened to spill out.

Mickey embraced her too, but stiffly. "I hope to see you again soon, Rachel."

"Yes," Rachel agreed. "Very soon."

It was Sue's turn. "Could you stay? Maybe it would help and I swear I won't ask you about Jeff."

The request took Rachel by surprise; she'd expected

to be the one asking Sue, though the subject of Sue's feelings for Todd seemed not at all urgent now. "I can stay. I believe a cup of espresso would do me good."

After Diane and Mickey left, Sue and Rachel settled back into their chairs. A busboy cleared away the dessert plates from the table. Then a waiter took their orders for coffee. The interlude gave Rachel a chance to collect herself a bit.

Once the waiter returned with their espresso, setting a delicate china cup in front of each of them, Sue leaned toward Rachel. "I've got something exciting to tell you. I only wish the timing was better."

Rachel took a sip from her cup. "What is it? That you've decided to move to New York?"

Sue gave a little laugh. "Possibly, yes, but it's much more than that. Rachel, I'm in love, madly in love."

Rachel almost dropped the cup in her hand. For a fleeting second she imagined Sue was about to confess that Todd was the object of her affections. Common sense—and one long look at Sue—said that couldn't be true.

"What's the matter, Rachel? Are you shocked speechless?" Sue laughed again. "It does happen, you know. People fall in love."

"I apologize, Sue. I mean I am surprised, but. . . . Who is he?"

"Well, I was going to tell everyone at lunch," Sue began, hedging, "but I was afraid of your reaction, yours and Mickey's, that is."

"Why? We'd be happy for you."

Sue ran a red-tipped finger along the rim of her cup. "Normally, I'd assume you'd be glad for me. But the night of the reunion I got the distinct impression that you and Mickey couldn't stand Rob—loathed him, in fact." She nervously bit her lip.

"Rob? You're in love with Rob Ransom?"

"Yes, and as thrilled as can be about it."

Rachel automatically rose from her chair and went over to embrace Sue. "I'm thrilled too, you crazy woman! But how? I mean, when?"

Sue grinned; her eyes sparkled. Rachel wondered why she hadn't noticed before. But then, she'd been preoccupied with her own dilemmas.

"How, I'm not really sure, Rachel. I suppose it's that old thing called chemistry. The when part is easy. It started at the reunion. You and Todd had already left when Rob invited me to dance. Afterward he asked me out."

"And the rest is history," Rachel finished for her. "Is that why you barely ate a bite from the buffet table?" She hoped it was the reason.

"Not exactly." Sue took a sip of her espresso. "That's another thing. I'd been sick." She held up her hand to halt Rachel's response. "I'm better now, much better," she emphasized.

"What was it, if you don't mind my asking? Something serious?"

"Kind of. Salmonella."

"Food poisoning."

Sue nodded. "It can be a nasty bug. I felt deathly ill for a while. I have a hunch I picked it up from potato salad I ate at a garden party. My appetite was gone for weeks, it seemed, but the food on the buffet table looked too delicious to pass up."

"And then you couldn't eat it." Rachel's notion that Sue was anorexic fled.

"An awful waste." Sue made a face. "Why don't we get back to a more pleasant subject?"

"Like Rob?"

"He's not flippant, honestly he's not." Sue put her hands out in a gesture of entreaty. "At the reunion he was trying to be entertaining. Even he admits he hammed it up too much. I wasn't going to, but I broke down and told him that you and Jeff had never married, that you'd broken up ages ago." She seemed to gauge Rachel's reaction, then went on, "He felt bad about what he'd said over the microphone. He's been wanting to make amends to you ever since."

"He has?" Rachel tried to picture a humble Rob Ransom. It was difficult. Still, she'd always known Sue to be levelheaded. If Sue thought Rob was a terrific guy, Rachel decided to take her word for it. "Tell Rob not to worry. He's forgiven."

"He'll be glad to hear that." Sue regarded Rachel carefully. "Are you sure you're all right? I realize I'm breaking my promise, but I want you to answer one question. Has Jeff threatened you in any way?"

"No." The answer came too quickly, though Rachel tried to look composed.

"Okay," Sue replied after a pause. "I'll accept that for now. You can be sure, though, I'll be checking on you soon." She set aside her coffee cup. "I have to apologize too for monopolizing Diane at lunch. It's just that Rob got signed for a major role in an off-Broadway play and he's been talking marriage and I've been considering it because we can't bear the idea of being eight hundred miles apart and—" She stopped, breathless and laughing.

Rachel smiled. Reaching for Sue's hand, she said, "I understand. Completely. And I think it's wonderful."

"Are you in love too, Rachel? With Todd Andrews?"

The sudden question was like a blow to Rachel, though she should have seen it coming. Her smile vanished; she averted her eyes to shield them from Sue's expectant gaze. How quickly circumstances had changed! "I am. I mean I was, but . . . "

Sue's response was swift—and much like Diane's.

"Gosh, I feel terrible, Rachel. I would never have asked if I'd had any idea things might not be going well."

Rachel met her friend's eyes. "They'd been going well, too well, it seems. Then yesterday we had a disagreement. More than that. I don't know what will happen now."

Sue's eyes reflected sympathy. "Couples do argue. They make up too. Don't give up hope. Unless you want to."

"I don't want to. At least I don't think I want to." A giggle escaped Rachel that sounded like a hiccup. She was on the verge of tears. "I'm not making any sense."

"You're making perfect sense—for someone who's in love," Sue said gently. "I had more than a crush on Todd once, if you remember."

"I do." Rachel didn't elaborate. There was no need to.

"A true case of unrequited feelings. Finally, I got smart and realized that Todd wasn't the one for me, that all I was doing was making myself miserable. But do you know something?"

"What?"

Sue reached over and took hold of Rachel's hand. "I believe with all my heart that Todd's the one for you."

A tear spilled down onto Rachel's cheek. She quickly wiped it away. "I wish I could too," she said.

The following Tuesday, Rachel was about to open the boutique when she saw Sammy walking her way. From his solemn expression, she guessed he had more to tell her about the impending sale of Penny Lane.

Fueled by three cups of strong coffee, Rachel's nerves were already on edge. After the disquieting events of recent days, how could she bear another piece of bad news? She tried to muster a brave smile. "Hello, Sammy."

He shook his head. "I've got some news, Rachel. Do you have a minute?"

"Of course. Come in." She fumbled with her keys, nearly dropping them before she got the door open.

Once inside, Sammy regarded her. "You look tired, Rachel. Are you all right?"

No use lying. "I haven't slept well for a few nights. I've had a lot on my mind." Seeing the genuine concern in his eyes, she hastened to add, "I'll be all right. Thanks for asking, Sammy."

He appeared doubtful. "Gee, maybe I should've waited, but I promised I'd let you know as soon as I heard anything on the Arcade."

"I want to know. The petition didn't succeed in convincing Mineola to keep Penny Lane?"

"Haven't heard on that yet. I wouldn't put a wager on it."

"There's still a chance then." She tried to inject a note of optimism into what seemed to be a hopelessly gloomy situation.

"A miracle could happen, I suppose." Sammy hesitated. "The bad news is that Will's found out who's planning to buy out Mineola."

A painful knot formed in Rachel's stomach. "Who?"

"Silverthorne."

"No!" she responded vehemently, as if she'd just been slapped. Sammy's eyebrows arched in surprise. "I mean, is Will sure?"

"As sure as can be. He got the news from a real reliable source." Sammy looked down at his folded hands. "If the deal goes through, Rachel, we can say good-bye to the fair deal we've had with Mineola, say good-bye too to our shops, I reckon."

"But maybe . . . " She frantically searched for a response—one that would somehow reassure them both that the name Silverthorne wasn't linked with impending economic disaster. "Couldn't it be possible that Silverthorne would leave Penny Lane as it is? The Arcade's filled to capacity with reliable tenants, and most are prospering. Besides, the whole building was renovated five years ago, wasn't it?"

Sammy gave her an indulgent smile. She knew he wasn't being condescending. He was too humble for that. But she felt foolish just the same. After a moment, he said, "What you say is true—that is, the part about the Arcade. From what I've heard, though, Silverthorne's got a reputation as a money-grabbing outfit. They're not apt to let things lie."

Rachel's legs went weak; she reached out to support herself on the nearby counter. Silverthorne. Out of all the property companies in the Twin Cities, why did it have to be the one Todd worked for that wanted Penny Lane?

She felt an unaccountable surge of anger toward Todd, as if he personally were to blame for the decision that could imperil her means of living as well as the livelihood of others. *Stop it,* she ordered herself silently. Just because she was cross with Todd over a personal matter didn't mean she had reason to indict him on this issue. Yet she realized that, all along, she had subconsciously feared it was A. Bradley Silverthorne who had designs on Penny Lane Arcade.

"Rachel?" Sammy's voice brought her back. "I sure hated to be the one to have to break this to you." He looked contrite. "I'm sorry if I spoiled your day."

Rachel touched his arm. "Don't apologize. We have to face this together, Sammy. We have to fight together too," she added with angry determination.

"Yes," he agreed, but he sounded tired.

She studied Sammy and thought of the hardships it would bring on him to lose his newspaper stand. He had a wife and three children to support.

"It looks like you've got a customer." Sammy gestured toward the door.

Rachel saw that the elderly customer making her way into the boutique was Regina Southworth. Helping her with her selections could take the better part of the morning. That meant further conversation with Sammy on the fate of Penny Lane would have to be postponed. But Rachel knew the topic would soon come up again, if not with Sammy then Meg, for they were to have lunch together the next day.

Sammy left with the promise that he would keep her posted on any other developments.

Despite her glumness, Rachel put on a smile for her patron. "Good morning, Mrs. Southworth," she said, noting how the older woman beamed when asked, "What can I help you with today?"

Rachel didn't have to wait for the next day, after all, to see Meg. Like an answer to a prayer, her friend appeared just as she was about to close up shop. But one look at Meg set off an alarm in Rachel's mind. More bad news, Meg's expression said clearly.

Without a greeting, Meg began, "We've got to talk."

"Sure, but weren't we getting together tomorrow?"

Meg took hold of Rachel's arm. "I can't. A meeting's been called and I have to be there. It'll probably last way into the night."

Meetings. Rachel was suddenly reminded that Todd had said he'd be tied up in meetings until Wednesday. Not that it mattered now. Since their parting Friday, she hadn't expected to hear from him anyway. To cover her despair, she said, "Is that the only thing realtors and developers do, attend meetings?"

Meg offered no witty answer, not even a smile. "After what I have to tell you, I doubt you'd be in the mood for lunch."

It's about Penny Lane, isn't it?'' Rachel asked, knowing intuitively it was. Meg acknowledged the question with a nod of her head. "I've been clued in. Sammy told me that Silverthorne is the company planning the takeover."

"Is that all you heard?"

Rachel's heart took a plunge. "There's more?"

"Yes. Can we go somewhere and talk?" Meg looked around the boutique as if she felt uncomfortable.

"How about Swartz's?" Swartz's was a neighborhood deli where the two friends sometimes met for a sandwich or fountain cream soda.

"Okay." Meg waited in silence while Rachel picked up her purse and secured Cabbage Rose's for the night.

Outside, the summer evening was hot and humid, and the sidewalk was jammed with commuters. Rachel drew in a deep breath; the air seemed to stick in her lungs and throat.

Meg took a few steps, stopping in front of the boutique's decorated window. Rachel stopped too. "You know, Cabbage Rose is a classy lady." Meg smiled, but her eyes still telegraphed trouble. "Just like you," she added softly to Rachel.

"Thank you," was all Rachel could think to say. She wondered if the time would soon come when Cabbage Rose would be forced to vacate the storefront window.

The two friends moved on, neither speaking until they reached Swartz's and were seated with their cream sodas at a corner table.

Meg took one sip of her drink and set it aside. "There's no easy way to say this, Rach."

"So tell me then."

"Sammy's right. Silverthorne is the buyer." She paused for a heartbeat. "But, according to Jason, Todd Andrews is the one Bradley's handpicked to redesign the Arcade."

Rachel went numb. "Todd? Redesign the Arcade?" she repeated dazedly.

Meg's hand reached out for hers. "I'm truly sorry," she whispered. "I knew that you were counting on me to relay whatever Jason learned. I was shocked myself to hear that Todd's on the project."

Rachel blinked, as if she'd just wakened from sleep— a nightmare. But this was real; what Meg told her was true. She had no doubt of that. For an instant she knew something very like hatred for Todd Andrews. "It's . . . all right," she stammered at last. "It doesn't matter, Meg."

"What do you mean? Aren't you and Todd—" She didn't finish the sentence. "Oh, Rach!" she cried.

"We had an argument." She told her friend everything that had happened the Friday before, and Saturday too. "It's for the best. It has to be." Rachel was sure she sounded totally unconvincing.

"Maybe Todd will turn Bradley down."

Hope flickered briefly in Rachel's heart, then waned. "No, I don't think so, Meg. You tried to warn me about Todd right from the beginning. I didn't listen."

"It wasn't Todd, remember?" Meg reminded gently. "I just wanted you to be aware of Silverthorne's reputation. My fear was that Todd would be so impressed with Bradley that he wouldn't be able to see the seamier qualities of the man and his company."

"And you were right. Bradley has blinded Todd, hasn't he? Enough that Todd doesn't fathom what Silverthorne's takeover will mean for Penny Lane's tenants . . . for me."

"Likely he doesn't. But he did have every right to get upset when you insisted on confronting Jeff alone."

"Did I hear right?"

"Of course. You love him, don't you, Rach?" she probed gently.

Rachel closed her eyes; all she could see were images of Todd. After a moment, she met Meg's gaze. "Sue asked me the same question. I think you know the answer."

"Then's there's still hope, Rach."

"I wish that were true."

"At least give Todd a chance to explain. Even a man accused of murder is innocent until proven guilty."

Rachel smiled a little. "All right. But I may not see Todd again."

Meg smiled too. "You will, Rach. You know why?" Rachel shook her head. "Because he's as desperately in love with you as you are with him. And, like me, he's determined not to let you come to any harm."

Chapter Ten

Wednesday and Thursday passed and Rachel heard nothing from Todd. *"He's as desperately in love with you as you are with him."* Meg's statement played through Rachel's mind as she went about the task of hanging up a new consignment of slacks and blouses.

It was after closing Thursday evening, and the thought of going home was unbearable to her. So she'd lingered at the boutique, creating tasks for herself. Around six o'clock the temptation had grown great to call Todd. She resisted the urge, determined that he should be the one to contact her first.

Besides, what would she say to him if she got through? Spring on him the news about Silverthorne and Penny Lane? Demand to know how he could allow himself to be involved in a project that was certain to send the tenants of the Arcade packing—and, oh by the way, that included her? Beg him to explain how he could cause her such grief when he'd passionately declared she was the reason for his happiness?

Suddenly it seemed as if nothing made sense to Rachel. Out of sheer frustration she grabbed a pair of slacks from the pile of clothes and threw them across the room.

The outburst did nothing to ease her frustration and, after a moment, she retrieved the slacks and placed them properly on a hanger. As she did so, she resolved not to think about Todd for the rest of the evening. She had a more urgent matter demanding her attention, and it would take every ounce of fortitude she could muster to carry out her plans. Tomorrow was Friday. Tomorrow was the day she would challenge Jeff.

"You are one-hundred-percent wrong if you believe I sent these," Jeff Martin said coldly and bluntly. He thrust in front of Rachel's face the pages she'd handed him a moment before.

She stood face-to-face with him in a hallway of the coroner's office. It was two o'clock on Friday afternoon. She hadn't planned to come so early, but she'd grown impatient and hadn't been able to make herself wait until later in the day. Nor had she taken time to go home and check for another communication from the stalker.

Jeff was clad in his work clothes, a white smock over sky-blue shirt and navy slacks. Covering his shoes were disposable slippers, like the kind doctors and nurses wore when performing surgery. Rachel considered that they gave his appearance an incongruous look.

Yet she couldn't deny that Jeff was an attractive man, even if there was now something about his features that struck her as shifty. The way he stared at her set her on edge.

Just like at the reunion, the newsstand, at Anthony's. How could she know if he was telling her the truth or whether it was all a perverted game to him?

If it was, she hoped she was prepared. She'd lain awake most of the night before plotting what she would say, how she would keep control of her feelings and not give in to an emotional outburst. So far, she'd succeeded. She'd had her say firmly, without a hint of hysteria.

Jeff thought that women were weak; he'd told her so on several occasions. Rachel had considered the remark worse than an insult. Today she was proving to him that she was strong. But as they eyed each other warily, she wondered what she should do next.

"You believe I'm lying," he said, breaking into her thoughts. "Don't flatter yourself, Rachel." His gaze held hers. "Long ago I accepted it was finished between us. And if you imagine I'm wasting away over you. . . . " He shook his head, as if the idea didn't dignify a response.

"Then why were you watching me at the reunion? At Sammy's newsstand? At Anthony's? Are you going to say I only dreamed that I saw you?"

Jeff took a step closer to her, shoving the sheets of paper back into her hand. "In the case of Anthony's, yes, you dreamed it." His jaw set in a familiar way. "I was nowhere near Anthony's at lunch or any other hour on Saturday. I was right here in the pathology lab the entire day, examining tissue samples in a homicide case."

A shiver went through Rachel. Whether it was because of Jeff's reference to his job, the notion of homicide, or because his alibi called into question her own integrity, she wasn't certain.

Jeff shoved his hands into the large pockets of his smock. "If you have doubts, be my guest and ask David Holmes, who assisted me. Incidentally, Dr. Holmes is Chief Medical Examiner for Ramsey County."

Rachel forced herself to look at him. "So maybe I was mistaken. Once. What about the other times?"

Just for an instant Jeff's eyes conveyed to her a turbulent and troubled signal, as though a tempest brewed beneath his outwardly calm exterior. Then his poise returned. "I admit I was watching you. Is that a federal offense, Rachel?"

She was instantly reminded of Lt. Savage's similar comment. "Watching someone is hardly a crime," he'd said. Finally, she replied, "No, not an offense, Jeff. Just very strange, I'd say."

"You're entitled to your opinions," he said sarcastically. Then, as if he'd lost interest in the conversation, he gazed down the hallway. "If that's all you wanted, I have to get back to work."

The subject seemed to be closed. Perhaps, she thought as he turned from her.

She watched him go. Halfway down the corridor, Jeff stopped. Glancing over his shoulder, he said, "By the way, in case you hadn't considered it, I'm in a serious relationship with someone too."

A serious relationship. So he had a girlfriend after all. Rachel turned the idea over in her mind as she saw him enter the double doorway at the end of the long hall. It was then she detected the faint, sickening odor of formaldehyde. Strange she hadn't noticed it before. Or was that just her imagination too?

Maybe it was only a peculiar coincidence that Rachel found nothing in her mailbox when she checked it later that afternoon. No plain envelope with her name and address typed neatly in the middle. No note to read and shudder over.

After her meeting with Jeff she wasn't sure whether to be relieved or anxious that the stalker hadn't followed his usual pattern of communicating with her.

Jeff's blunt declaration that he was innocent of her charges had affected her more than she wanted to admit.

And the way he had treated her, his announcement that he was in a relationship, seemed to negate any suspicion of him she might have had. Almost.

If he'd told her the truth, she'd wasted a lot of mental energy on him when she should have been looking elsewhere for clues. What about the other suspects she and Meg had come up with? Sue was out, though Rachel had never seriously considered that she might be the guilty party. But there was Sidney. And Kerrie.

Kerrie—who had designs on Todd, who it appeared would stop at nothing to win his attention. Rachel wondered if Kerrie had gotten wind that there was a rift between Todd and herself. If so, Kerrie wouldn't waste time in making a move on Todd.

Rachel was at once consumed by the idea that Kerrie could be the one bent on frightening her. Messages had come on the past three Fridays; today there'd been none. Presuming Kerrie had sent the notes, she might see no need to continue. For the object of Todd's affections, Rachel herself, wasn't considered a threat anymore. It made perfect sense. If Kerrie was the stalker.

It was the "if" that bothered Rachel. There was no way to be certain. Yet. All she could do was stay alert and open to every possibility. She must. Her peace of mind, perhaps even her life, depended on it.

Meg dropped by Rachel's apartment on Saturday, anxious for news. As they sat together on the sofa, Rachel told of her encounter with Jeff, confessing that she wasn't completely convinced of his innocence. "But I can't help wondering if Kerrie is the culprit instead." She told Meg why she suspected Kerrie.

"It makes sense, Rach." Meg paused for a moment. "You haven't heard from Todd?"

Rachel cast her eyes downward. Her hand went to her neck, fingers touching the delicate chain of gold and pearls secured there. She hadn't taken it off since she and Todd had last been together. Maybe the time had come to put the necklace away.

"Your silence says a lot," Meg said softly.

Rachel set her gaze on a painting on the far wall of the living room. It was a watercolor of a sailboat at sea. The picture suggested tranquility. "I'm afraid he won't make contact first, Meg."

"Then why don't you?"

Rachel turned to her friend in surprise. "You mean I should call Todd?"

"Yes. Remember, you're the one who told Todd you needed time to mull things over. Maybe he feels you would resent it if he took the initiative. Or maybe he surmises you haven't heard about Silverthorne's intended buyout of Penny Lane or of his involvement in the project. He might not know how to tell you, Rach."

"But you yourself said that I would hear from him soon."

Meg gave her a rueful smile. "People in love don't always use rational judgment."

Rachel considered the mild censure was directed at her as much as Todd. "Okay. I'll call him. And by the way, Meg, have I mentioned that you're the most persuasive person I've ever met?"

"Oh, once or twice." Meg laughed; for the first time in days, Rachel laughed too.

Meg left shortly after and Rachel found that she felt considerably better than she had before her friend's visit. She'd promised Meg that she would phone Todd, but she hadn't said when. She decided on the next evening, which would be Sunday. That would give her a chance to think through what she would say to him.

Having made up her mind on the matter, Rachel at once discovered she was bone tired. Maybe tonight she would finally be able to get some sleep.

* * *

Rachel slept, but she awoke with a start. Her heart was thumping loudly and she was aware of what had caused it. She had dreamed again about the stalker. Only this time it wasn't Jeff she was afraid of. She didn't know who the stalker was for she couldn't see anyone, just a shadow looming in front of her.

Someone else was in the dream too, reaching out to snatch her from the danger ahead. But was the person a man or a woman? Could it have been Meg? Sue? Todd? She had no idea.

Getting out of bed, Rachel remembered something else—the stalker's last message. *"I'm your shadow, the darkness that haunts you."* Now the stalker's ominous words were coming true, and suddenly her usually warm and cheery bedroom seemed dismal and cold. Rachel went to her closet. She took out her ragged fleece robe, the one she donned on winter mornings or when she was ill and in need of comfort. She wrapped it snugly around herself.

Rachel wore the robe all day, not bothering to change until early evening when she decided to make a trip to the grocery. She didn't buy much, just some fruit, cheese, and milk. Though the parking garage beneath her building was well lit, she got the jitters as she walked from her car to the underground elevator entrance. Several times she glanced nervously over her shoulder.

She was alone on the elevator, and the hallway appeared vacant when she got out on the eighth floor. Just the same she hurried to her apartment and wasted no time letting herself in.

Was this how it would always be, she wondered, turning the deadbolt on her door with trembling hands. If she never learned the identity of who stalked her, would she forever be a prisoner of her own paranoia, constantly vigilant, searching for a face whose eyes were fixed on her?

Rachel found it impossible to dismiss the question as she put her few groceries away. When she almost dropped the carton of milk, she noticed her palms were sweaty. She quickly dried them and made up her mind to try Todd's number.

She didn't reach him, only his answering machine. She hung up without leaving a message. Immediately after, her phone rang. It was Sue, saying she'd been worried about her. Once more Rachel recounted the past week's events.

"Would you like me to come over, Rachel? I could. I'd like to. Or we could meet somewhere for coffee."

The suggestion was tempting, but Rachel couldn't bear the idea of going out again. "That's sweet of you, really it is, Sue," she said at last. "I'm just not in the mood to do anything. I've decided to get in touch with Todd this evening."

"I can't begin to tell you how much I want things to work out for you," Sue responded over the line. "I'll be sending lots of positive thoughts your way, Rachel. Lots of protective ones too."

"Thanks, Sue. I could use them."

"Speaking of things that are positive, Rob and I are going to be married next week."

Rachel gripped the phone tighter. "No! Getting married? That's fantastic." Her voice faltered slightly. "Where? In St. Paul?"

"Unfortunately not. Rob's already in New York for rehearsal of the play. He's coming back for me Wednesday and we'll fly out together and say our vows there."

"So you're moving to New York. Won't I see you again?"

"You'll see me, I promise. We'll make a fast trip to St. Paul as soon as he gets a break. I have to pack up

most of my worldly goods and ship them to New York.
But we'll be making plenty of visits home.''

"You'd better.''

They said good-bye and Rachel hung up the phone.
She wanted so much to be excited for Sue. She couldn't
and felt sad over it. She was pleased that Sue had found
true love, but the notion of weddings and happily-ever-
afters seemed at the moment as remote to her as the
moon.

Two more tries brought no response from Todd other
than the recorded message on his machine. The sound
of his voice only served to heighten her despair. On her
last attempt, Rachel left a message for him to return her
call. After that there was nothing more to be done but
contend with the misery encompassing her heart.

Rachel would have been hard pressed to say just how
she got through the next couple of days. She went about
her usual routine, but without color or feeling.

She smiled automatically whenever she greeted a customer at the boutique. She chatted with Mrs. Southworth
about the loveliness of the weather lately and laughed
when Mrs. Peniman, another regular at the store, relayed
a humorous anecdote about her Yorkshire terrier.

But the smiles, the small talk, were hollow, merely
acts staged for whoever was her audience at the moment.
The only time any emotion stirred in Rachel was when
the phone rang. She would give a small jump, then make
herself wait four rings before picking up the receiver.
She didn't want Todd to think she was dying to hear
from him—even if she was.

None of the calls were from Todd though, and by
Tuesday evening, Rachel almost wished her phone
would never ring again. As she slumped on the sofa,
filled with weariness, she wondered if she should take
her vacation early this year and visit her parents now

instead of waiting until September. Maybe if she got away for a while she could begin to put her life into some sort of perspective.

She worked the idea over in her mind as she prepared for bed. She thought of San Francisco, the way it might look at this time of year. She'd been there once during the summer and had loved standing on the portico of her parents' home at dawn to watch the fog roll in, all gray and gloomy, over the bay.

The images of San Francisco conjured in her mind began to relax her. Then the telephone jangled and all the tension returned as she rushed to answer it.

Taking a deep breath, she said, "Hello?"

"Rach?"

"Oh, hi, Meg." She tried not to sound disappointed.

"Are you all right, Rach? You sound like you've just run a race."

Rachel sat down on the bed. "I'm okay."

"You don't seem very sure." There was a pause. "You haven't heard from Todd, have you?"

"How did you guess?"

Meg gave a short, humorless laugh. "Not a guess. That's why I'm calling. I heard some news today about Silverthorne, and about Todd."

Rachel straightened, sensing the news was bad. "What, Meg?"

"Well, first of all, none of this is confirmed yet, but the scoop is that Bradley's in major trouble. He's about to be indicted on charges of bribery. It has something to do with obtaining permits for a resort Silverthorne's planning to build on the lake."

Rachel gasped. "Todd told me about the resort. But not much." She braced herself for the rest. "What about Todd?"

"Oh, Rach, he's not in trouble. Nothing like that." Meg was the one who sounded breathless now. "But you remember I'd been having Jason do a bit of detective work concerning Silverthorne?''

"Yes.''

"He told me just this morning that there's also a big shake-up going on at Silverthorne and Todd may be leaving the company. By his own wishes, not Bradley's,'' she stressed.

Rachel was speechless, stunned for a moment by Meg's report. "He's quitting his job?'' she said at last.

"Remember, Rach, nothing is confirmed, but yes, it appears he's going to quit. Not only that, Jason heard that Todd's been out of town lately. No one seems to know where. But that would explain why he hasn't contacted you.''

It explained a lot of things, Rachel thought—and brought a hundred other questions to mind. "Thanks, Meg. Thanks for telling me. I feel like . . . like I'm in a trance of some kind. But I want you to keep me informed, no matter how bad the news might be.''

"I firmly believe the next person you'll hear anything from will be Todd. But, yes, whatever information Jason passes on, you'll be the first to know.''

"I appreciate that, Meg.''

"Have you gotten . . . has the stalker contacted you again?''

"Not so far.''

"Then maybe it was Kerrie. But, Rach . . . ''

"What?''

"Take care just the same. It may not be over yet.''

Rachel prayed it was as she promised once more, "Yes, I'll be careful.''

Chapter Eleven

As absurd as the idea seemed, Rachel speculated that Todd had gone off to Acapulco on the modeling assignment Kerrie had so "generously" told him about. Hadn't he said the notion might appeal to him under particular circumstances?

Perhaps he'd concluded that his life at the moment warranted a sudden and major change. What could be more contradictory to his usual routine than posing for pictures on sparkling sands beside an azure sea? And what could take his mind off his woes more favorably than the attentions of a certain flirtatious model—Kerrie, to be exact?

The vision summoned up in Rachel's mind made her anger flare. She tried to calm herself by reasoning that it wasn't logical Todd would take off without having the courtesy to offer her some explanation—if it was true that he loved her.

Absorbed in her inner debate, she almost missed the

knock at her door. After a light dinner earlier that evening, she'd retired to the balcony where she'd spent considerable time mulling over her predicament.

There was another knock, a sharp one this time. Rachel got to her feet and went inside. She squinted through the peephole of her front door. A man clad in a cap and uniform stood on the other side. He was holding a vase of flowers. "Yes?" she asked, sure he must have the wrong apartment.

"Blume's Floral here with a delivery for Miss Anders."

She opened the door to him and discovered that the flowers were roses. Crimson roses nestled among shiny green leaves and baby's breath. The vase was of cut glass. The man handed it to her and she murmured, "Thank you," her eyes still fixed on the bouquet. She shut the door without hearing the delivery man's response.

The vase was slightly wet, so Rachel carried it through to the kitchen and set it on the counter. She stood there a moment, admiring the lovely arrangement, her thoughts on Todd. Suddenly she felt in a charitable mood. It might be true that he'd gone away without calling her, but now he was letting her know in a most wonderful way how much she meant to him.

She looked for a card, but didn't spot it immediately. He must have included one, she reasoned. After a bit of detective work, she found it tucked well down in the lush greenery. With care she lifted the small card out and unfolded it.

The note inside was not the loving one she anticipated. There was a message, all right. It ran over the card in black ink, the lines crooked, the words a mess of interconnecting spikes and loops. She had seen that writing before.

Her eyes were drawn to the name at the bottom. She

drew in a sharp breath and flung the card down on the counter as if it were in flames. This couldn't be happening. But it was. Her eyes hadn't been mistaken.

With dreaded expectation, she made herself retrieve the card and read its message.

Did you remember, Rachel? Did you remember our special day is tomorrow? I sent the flowers early so that you would think of me. You wouldn't forget our special day, would you, Rachel?

Sidney W.

Sidney Wetherly. Why had she been so dense? Why hadn't she accepted before what was the obvious truth? His fixation on her through high school. Her bizarre encounter with him at the reunion. The jealousy he must have felt when he saw her with Todd. Then the cryptic messages he'd sent under the guise of anonymity. Now a bouquet of roses with his name attached.

It all came together like some morbidly fascinating puzzle. And Rachel herself was the last critical piece, the one Sidney was determined to make fit.

Rachel stared at the flowers. The crimson petals looked more the color of blood, the leaves waxy and artificial. Trembling, she grabbed up the vase so fast that it nearly slipped through her fingers. Opening the cabinet door under the sink, she took out a trash bag from a box she kept there. Rachel hurled the vase, flowers first, into the bag and secured it shut. Then she headed with the bundle to the building's trash compactor.

During the night the wind blew in a rainstorm and it continued, without letup, the next day. Rachel decided to take the bus to work rather than drive, even though it meant a two-block walk from the bus stop to the boutique. Was it because she didn't want to face returning to the garage under her building that evening and make the walk alone from her car to the elevator?

Regardless, she told herself she enjoyed being out in the rain, that the change of pace would be good for her. Even though she was a half hour late opening up, there were no customers waiting.

The hours dragged by as the rain and wind made for a blustery day. For once, Rachel was glad business was off. She couldn't concentrate on her tasks as it was, but she tried to occupy herself doing markdowns on consignments. Her mind was attempting to figure out why Sidney considered this their ''special day'' and what she should do now that she was sure he was the one stalking her.

Reason dictated that she should immediately inform Lt. Savage; a part of her rebelled against the notion. At the same time, she regretted having disposed of the vase of flowers and note. The lieutenant might consider them incriminating evidence.

Rachel thought of confronting Sidney, as she had Jeff. Or she could consult with Meg, get her friend's advice. No. Meg was likely to come on the run if she called, and she didn't want that.

Perhaps she was making more of Sidney's attentions than she should be. He was definitely strange, but he'd always been like that. In the past, he'd never done anything to her that had suggested he was dangerous. Maybe he simply cared for her, loved her in his own odd way, and hoped that someday she would care for him too.

Back and forth her mind played mental Ping-Pong until it was closing time. Outside, the sky had grown progressively darker. Rachel buttoned her raincoat and fitted on the waterproof hat she'd worn that morning in lieu of lugging an umbrella.

When she stepped out onto the sidewalk, she saw wisps of fog curling like ghostly arms around the tops

of the tall buildings. It was still raining, though the wind
had died away.

She had a few minutes before catching her bus, so she
made a stop at Sammy's newsstand for a paper.

"Did anyone ever tell you you're even more beautiful
when it rains? Puts color in your cheeks."

Sammy's compliment, given with a wink and a grin,
made Rachel smile. "And did anyone ever mention that
you're a flatterer, Sammy?"

His grin widened, then he grew serious. "No more
news yet," he volunteered.

He didn't have to specify just what news he meant.
Rachel understood. She opened her mouth to relay what
she'd heard from Meg of Silverthorne's troubles. Then
she thought better of it.

"You were gonna say something, Rachel?"

Avoiding his eyes, she muttered, "Nothing except that
I'm keeping my fingers crossed."

"I expect we all are."

Rachel took the paper from him in exchange for her
money and started off with a "See you later, Sammy."

There were few people on the street as she walked in
the direction of the bus stop. She hadn't gone far when
she heard someone say her name. Believing it was
Sammy, she turned back—and found herself staring into
the blank face of Sidney.

Rachel began to tremble. For a moment, she feared
she would scream. It was like her nightmare. She was
confronting the man who stalked her—and she couldn't
doubt his identity.

"Rachel?" Sidney's mouth was set in a frown. He
wore an ancient-looking gray slicker and a droopy hat
whose brim came down over his forehead, nearly con-
cealing his eyes. His dark hair was plastered to his
cheeks. The effect was repulsive.

"What do you want?" She meant to sound defiant,

but the high pitch of her voice must have emboldened him.

With a swift gesture, he pulled back the brim of his hat so that his eyes met hers. Before she could think to stop him, his hand came up to grip her arm. "Aren't you going to thank me, Rachel? You liked them, didn't you?"

Rachel's tongue flicked over her lips. "You mean the roses?" She strove for civility when all she wanted to do was demand that he get out of her life. "They were pretty," she said at last. "But I can't talk now. I have a . . . an appointment."

"Cancel it," he said harshly. "This is our anniversary, or don't you remember that either?" He began to tug on her arm to take her with him.

"What do you think you're doing?" Panic rose in her as she tried to yank free from him.

His hold on her tightened. "I want you to have dinner with me. Tonight."

"I told you, Sidney, I can't." Rachel glanced feverishly around her for a sign of a policeman. Just the sight of a blue uniform might serve to deter Sidney. But no officer was to be seen. Only several people passed by, all of them carrying umbrellas, their heads ducked underneath against the rain. None of them paid her any heed.

Giving a violent jerk, she pulled free from Sidney and began to run in the direction of the bus stop.

She heard him behind her, shouting. She didn't look around, but sensed he was coming after her. The heavy fall of his footsteps sounded like thunder in her ears. Or was it the terrible pounding of her heart?

Half a block up she felt a splash of water and peered toward the curb. A vehicle had drawn alongside her, easing to a stop. It was a sports car, sleek and red, the windows tinted black. For some reason Rachel paused, and she saw her bus go past. There was no possibility of catching it now. Another one wouldn't be by for half an hour.

Then the passenger door of the car opened. Someone addressed her. In disbelief, Rachel bent over and gazed into the car's dark interior.

Chapter Twelve

"Mickey!"

"Surprised?" Mickey looked delighted. "I saw you and thought you were in a hurry. Why don't you get in, Rachel?"

Rachel couldn't believe the incredible timing. Glancing behind, she saw that Sidney had almost caught up with her.

"What's the matter?"

Mickey's question drew her back. At that moment, she felt the touch of Sidney's hand on her arm and heard his voice, rasping and wheezy from running, pleading with her to wait. Rachel made up her mind. She climbed into Mickey's car and slammed the door shut.

She stared through the window at her pursuer as Mickey started to pull away from the curb. All at once, Sidney's hand came up against the window, hitting the glass, and Rachel let out a cry of alarm.

"Don't worry. He can't get in."

The click of the power lock on Rachel's door swiftly backed up Mickey's promise.

She was safe. But for how long? Rachel sagged down in the cushioned seat, closing her eyes. "Sidney's the one who's been after me, not Jeff," she told Mickey softly.

When Mickey made no reply, Rachel went on, "You probably think I'm crazy, but . . ." Her words trailed off as the car picked up speed, tires squealing on the wet pavement. She was too tired to offer further explanation.

"I don't think you're crazy." There was a pause. "Just a little dense."

Rachel's eyes opened in surprise at the odd remark. She looked at her friend. Mickey was smiling. The notion occurred to Rachel that it was the coldest smile she'd ever seen. She shuddered, then promptly scolded herself for being too sensitive. After all, her uneasiness had nothing to do with Mickey.

Still . . . "What do you mean, Mickey, that I'm a little dense?"

"I mean this."

There was a gleam of something in the dim light. Rachel's gaze was drawn to Mickey's hand. An expression of horror must have shown on her face.

Mickey gave a laugh, but there was no humor in it. "You *are* surprised," she said at last.

Rachel stared in disbelief at the gun clutched in Mickey's hand. It was a small revolver, and its shiny, snub-nosed barrel was pointed at her ribs. Instinctively, she shrunk away from the weapon. There was no place to retreat as she came up hard against the door.

"Don't think of trying to escape. I locked it, remember?"

Rachel made herself let go of the door handle. How had she ended up caught like a bird in a trap? "Mickey, I don't understand." Her voice quaked. She imagined she was dreaming again, a nightmare more wild and senseless than any she'd had before.

Mickey was observing her sideways, steering with her left hand as she weaved in and out of traffic on the rain-slicked street. "You wouldn't understand. You thought it had to be Jeff. Then it was Sidney," she said mockingly. "*Now* who do you think sent you those warnings?"

"It was you, wasn't it, Mickey? But why? Why would you do something like that? We're friends!"

"Friends?" Mickey shook her head. "Come on, Rachel. We were friends only in your fantasies. I was always the odd woman out. Poor fat helpless Mickey. The fringe element of your nice little group. And the one you just had to make your own pet project."

Rachel could make no reply, for wasn't Mickey telling the truth? Yet she hoped that if she could keep Mickey talking, there might be some way to reason with her, or dissuade her, or unnerve her and then grab the gun. "Were you trying to get even?"

Mickey made a jolting turn to the right. The tires screeched and scraped against the curb. "You're over-simplifying. You always did."

Rachel heard Mickey, but her mind was distracted by what she saw out the window. They were headed away from the downtown business area and into an old factory district called Riverton. The streets, lined mostly with abandoned, windowless buildings, eventually ended at the river's edge in a hapless maze of rotting wharves and docks. It was a place haunted by derelicts and drug dealers, a place of danger and sudden violence.

As if to emphasize the fact, a siren wailed somewhere in the distance. Rachel glanced over her shoulder.

"Don't concern yourself, Rachel. It was an ambulance, going the other direction."

"Where are you taking me?" Rachel demanded with more authority than she felt capable of.

"Does it matter? Don't you want to know why I've been stalking you?" Mickey sounded accusing.

Stalking. Mickey had uttered the word first. All at once it came together in Rachel's mind as she recalled something Diane had said. "It's Todd, isn't it? You want him. And you think I'm standing in your way."

Mickey smirked at her. "You're a lot smarter than I thought."

Rachel winced as Mickey pressed the gun into her side. "If it's Todd you want, you don't need to hold me captive. Todd and I are . . . we're not seeing each other anymore." How did she herself know that it was a fact? No matter, it was obvious to Rachel that Mickey needed the kind of help she wasn't qualified to give. For now, she had little choice but to play along with Mickey's bizarre game.

"Very convenient, Rachel, but I don't believe you." Mickey sighed. "Life was always too easy for you. You were pretty, you were popular, you could have any guy you desired."

Easy. Rachel remembered those last torturous months with Jeff. "It wasn't as glamorous as you imagine."

Mickey glared at her. "Come on. Don't play on my sympathies. I saw the look of shock on your face when we first met at the reunion. You'd never dreamed that I could be attractive."

Rachel started to deny the charges, but then kept silent.

"And you, Sue, Diane—all of you were patronizing me, gushing over me, telling me I should be with Rob Ransom." Mickey's face flushed with rage. "All I wanted was for Todd to notice me, to realize that I was the woman who could make him happy." Her voice shook. "He was all I ever wanted. Then you took him away from me!"

"I didn't take him away. I'd never intentionally do anything like that to a friend. He came up and asked me to dance. You know that as well as I do."

"You don't get it, do you, Rachel? Privileged people never appreciate how lucky they are. I had to teach you a lesson. Don't you understand that? I had to."

Rachel saw beneath the tough exterior and sensed that Mickey too was vulnerable—and as frightened as she was. "No, I don't understand," she responded gently. "I can't fathom you getting pleasure from threatening me with messages that—"

"That kept you awake at night," Mickey cut in. "That gave you the feeling someone was watching every move you made. Aren't you curious about the Shakespeare?"

Keep her talking, Rachel told herself. "Yes, I was. I am. I'd forgotten about it until Todd reminded me. I showed him the messages, Mickey."

"It figures he would remember you reciting that poem. I hadn't, until a few days before the reunion. I was leafing through an old *Windjammer* and ran across a couple of pages on the Elizabethan Festival. How I hated that nonsense!"

Mickey paused, as if she was uncertain where she was going. Then she made another abrupt turn onto a narrow, trash-littered street.

"Anyway, you were in one of the pictures. There was a caption below it. But the photographer caught someone else in the photo too. Unintentionally, I'm sure."

"Who?" Rachel searched her memory for some recollection of the picture. She came up blank.

Mickey gave a sardonic laugh. "You shouldn't act so puzzled, Rachel. It was Todd standing just offstage, looking starry-eyed at you. I've told you already that he was nuts about you, but you didn't believe me.''

Rachel believed Mickey now. She'd heard the words from Todd himself, though to say so might provoke Mickey further.

''Back then I was smart enough to know I didn't stand a chance with Todd. A couple of years ago, after I dropped a hundred pounds, guys started paying attention to me. I didn't give a hoot about them. It was always Todd. I thought if I could find some way to see him again, he'd want me.'' She sighed. ''Eventually the reunion came along. I didn't care if he was married to Stacey. I wasn't going to let anything, or anyone, stand in my way,'' she said in a voice as hard as steel.

Mickey hesitated, her gaze reverting suddenly to the rearview mirror. She spat out a curse and, without warning, slammed on the brakes, nearly sending the car into a spin.

Rachel screamed. Mickey yelled for her to shut up. Trembling, Rachel clutched the door handle as the car lurched down a different street.

''Someone's following us!'' Mickey shrieked.

Rachel tried to look around. Mickey ordered her to keep her eyes straight ahead. She wondered if Mickey was hallucinating. The fog was thicker in this area; it rolled down the street in waves. Rachel knew they must be very near the river. Perhaps Mickey had actually seen a car come up behind and, in her unbalanced state, feared its driver was after her. Or had her reckless driving caught the eye of a vigilant patrolman?

All at once Mickey changed direction again and the car roared into an alleyway. A great curtain of fog hung just in front of them, hiding what lay beyond. As they sped toward it, the curtain seemed to part. Too late, Mickey must have seen the wall that loomed at the end of the alley.

"Stop!" Rachel cried. She closed her eyes; her body went rigid in anticipation of a crash.

But they didn't crash. There was a horrendous squealing of brakes. The car fishtailed wildly and ground to a stop just short of the wall.

The first thing Rachel saw when she opened her eyes was the gun being waved in her face.

"Get out!" Mickey commanded.

Dazed, Rachel tried the door; it was unlocked. She climbed out, and Mickey appeared at her side.

The exact sequence of what happened next would remain a blur in Rachel's mind. There was the acrid smell of burnt rubber in the air, and car exhaust. There was the sound of a man's voice calling her name, then Mickey's, with urgency. There was Mickey's arm clutching her in a stranglehold, and herself struggling in vain to get free. There was the gun now pressed to the flesh of her neck.

There was another car, just as Mickey had claimed. It was stopped just short of hers; the beam of its headlights cut the fog and its motor was running. There was the cry of a siren, and it seemed to be drawing nearer, not retreating.

A man stepped out from the mist. Rachel heard her name again, and Mickey's. The desperate, familiar ring of it rid her mind of the confusion. Her own response was without thought, born of a need deeper than her fear for herself. "Todd!" She groaned his name. He took a step forward, and she saw him clearly. "Stay back! Please stay back!" she cried.

"Don't come any closer," Mickey ordered. "I'll shoot."

There was a small click next to Rachel's ear; she knew Mickey had cocked the gun.

"Put the gun down, Mickey. There's no need for that now." Todd's request sounded calm, reasoning. "I'm here." His hand came up slowly, extended toward Mickey. "Isn't that what you wanted?"

"Wanted?" she echoed.

"Yes." He took another cautious step. "I have to apologize. I was a fool not to see how much you cared for me, how much I care for you."

Rachel listened, stunned, for a moment. Then Todd's eyes met hers. She understood what he was doing and felt the love and strength he projected to her.

She felt Mickey's uncertainty too. The pressure of the revolver against her neck lessened, as if the gun might be withdrawn.

"Trust me, Mickey," Todd said softly. "You know you can."

"I . . . don't know."

Sudden flashes of red and blue light illumined the fog. The scream of the once-distant siren reverberated through the alleyway. Then it was as if all havoc broke loose.

Mickey gripped Rachel tighter, the revolver brandished at Rachel's head. "I'll shoot!" she yelled over the sound of the dying siren. "Don't come any closer!"

She started to drag Rachel with her, but Todd was faster. He lunged for Mickey and the gun. Suddenly, Mickey rounded on him, still holding on to Rachel.

"No!" Rachel gasped, believing Mickey had gone over the edge, that in her desperation she was capable of turning on the man she claimed to love.

An order to halt was shouted through a bullhorn. Rachel saw a blue uniform, the gleam of a badge. But there was no time to lose. Rachel lifted her arm as high as she could, then thrust it downward with a great force. Her elbow made crunching contact with Mickey's ribs. Mickey let out a stunned cry.

Sensing Mickey was off balance, Rachel pushed mightily against her side. There was a loud clatter. When she looked, Rachel saw the gun had dropped to the pavement.

Mickey was doubled over, writhing in pain.

Todd grabbed the weapon and held it on Mickey, though it didn't seem necessary.

Two policemen appeared on the scene at once. They flanked Mickey on either side. Todd kept the revolver for a moment. Then he handed it over to a third officer who had come on the run. Rachel immediately recognized the officer as Lt. Savage.

Todd said something to the lieutenant that she couldn't hear. From one of the patrol cars a two-way radio crackled with static.

The next thing Rachel knew, Todd took her in his arms. She clung to him, and he held her so fiercely she could scarcely breathe. Despite herself, tears filled her eyes.

"It's all right," Todd whispered, burying his face in her hair for a moment. His mouth moved over her forehead, her cheek, at last taking her lips in a brief, intense kiss. "I love you." He murmured the words over and over against her mouth until at last she was able to compose herself and let go her death grip on him.

The three officers were occupied with Mickey, though Rachel was certain they would want to question Todd and herself. There were a few questions she longed to ask too, but only one mattered now. "How did you know?" It was still difficult to believe Todd was with her.

He smiled down at her, his eyes reflecting her gratitude. "I got lucky. Thank goodness, I got lucky." He reached in the pocket of the windbreaker he wore and brought out a piece of paper. He handed it to her.

The page was blank except for several lines typed in the middle. There was just enough light for Rachel to read the words of Shakespeare printed there, more lines of the poem Mickey had sent her. But it was the last part of the message that left Rachel weak.

Don't you know how long I've loved you, Todd? Don't you understand that Rachel could never love you like I love you? Don't you realize that she is standing in the way of our happiness?

Rachel's eyes were drawn to Mickey. She saw that Mickey was watching her and Todd. But Mickey's face was expressionless and her hands were behind her back. She'd been handcuffed.

"I found the envelope in my mailbox today," Todd said, bringing Rachel's attention back to him. "I'd just gotten home . . . from a trip. As soon as I saw it, I knew it had to be a message like the ones you'd received."

"You realized it was from Mickey?"

"No, but it was obvious to me that whoever was stalking you had to be a woman. That eliminated Jeff. And Sidney." He gave her a rueful look. "I thought it was Kerrie. Then I checked with her agency and was told she was in Acapulco and had been for over a week."

Rachel couldn't help saying, "I thought that's where you were. In Acapulco. Meg told me you were out of town."

Hurt must have shown on her face, for Todd cupped her chin in his hands and gazed deeply into her eyes.

"I was a long way from Mexico, and I have much to tell you, Rachel, but not right now."

"You didn't answer my original question. How did you determine Mickey was stalking me?"

"I wouldn't have, but I believed you were in danger. I was on my way to Cabbage Rose's when I saw you on the street. You were with some . . . a man." This time Todd looked uncertain.

"That was Sidney. I thought he was the stalker. He sent me roses and said today was our special day. He frightened me, Todd."

Todd shook his head. "Sidney. He's another puzzle." He paused. "Anyway, as I was saying, I started to pull up to the curb when you began to run. I followed in my car. Before I could find a spot to pull over and catch you, another car had come along."

"Mickey's."

"I watched as you got in and, on a hunch, followed. I wasn't about to let you out of my sight."

"I'm so grateful you didn't." From the corner of her eye, Rachel saw Lt. Savage approaching. "But how did he know, Todd?" she asked, indicating the officer.

"It didn't take me long to figure out something serious was going on. I called him on my car phone."

Rachel turned to the lieutenant. He acknowledged her. "Miss Anders, we'll need to take statements from you and Mr. Andrews at the precinct. Are you up to that now?"

She looked at Todd. He gave her an encouraging smile. "Yes, I believe I am, Lt. Savage." As Todd took hold of her hand and they followed the lieutenant back to his car, she doubted she'd ever be able to sort out the nightmarish experience she had just been through. Then she realized that she had much to be grateful for—most of all the presence of the man she loved at her side.

The next evening Todd took Rachel to the roof garden of Henley Plaza. They stood, arms wrapped cozily around each other, in the same spot where they'd kissed the night of the reunion. The fog and rain were gone, leaving behind a cloudless sky. Above, the bright sliver of a new moon hung suspended over the horizon. Below, the combined lights of the Twin Cities shone with amazing brilliance.

Rachel inhaled deeply. How sweet and clean the air smelled after a storm! For the last twenty-four hours she and Todd were either at the precinct station or sleeping exhaustedly at their respective apartments. From her own lingering weariness and the dark hollows under Todd's eyes, it seemed neither of them would soon be rested from their ordeal.

Yet she felt a clear sense of anticipation in Todd, in herself as well. She knew the time was right for him to speak his mind, though she broke the silence first. ''I wonder what will happen to Mickey.''

Todd looked out over the magnificent view. ''We have to believe she'll be given fair treatment.''

Rachel considered this. Lt. Savage had shared with them two shocking revelations about Mickey. First, the discovery that the gun she'd brandished had no bullets in it. Second, that she had left long, rambling suicide notes in her apartment and the glove compartment of her car.

''It's obvious she needs help instead of a jail sentence.''

''Yes,'' Todd agreed. His eyes met hers. ''We've got to trust the judicial system to recognize that. Right now Mickey is a danger to herself and others.''

''Sidney needs help too,'' Rachel said quietly.

''He's already receiving it.''

Rachel was stunned by the piece of news. ''What do you mean?''

''I mean that I was worried he'd keep harassing you, frightened that he might try to harm you. I called the cab company where he works. I was going to confront him.'' Todd smiled a little. ''His dispatcher told me Sidney had taken a leave. I insisted it was vital that I get in contact with him. The dispatcher hedged, then said Sidney had been admitted to a hospital. Charter East.''

Charter East was a well-known St. Paul psychiatric facility. "Thank goodness," was all Rachel could say.

Todd's hands came up to gently grasp her shoulders. "We have to talk, Rachel. Not about Mickey or Sidney or Kerrie or Jeff. About us. About our future."

"*Our future*," he'd said. Her heart accelerated noticeably. "I know," she replied.

"You mentioned you thought I'd been in Acapulco. I was in Seattle."

She was surprised again. "Seattle?"

He smiled. "Yes. I assume Meg also told you that I was leaving Silverthorne."

"She said that was the rumor. She also said Bradley had picked you to redesign Penny Lane . . . after his company purchases it."

"You heard that, huh?" Todd dropped his hands and stepped away from her. He gazed past her as he spoke. "I made a mistake, Rachel. I thought Bradley was giving me a great opportunity when he offered me the position with Silverthorne. I was ambitious. I am ambitious," he amended, "and I didn't want to believe the nasty stuff that was circulating about Bradley and his company."

"But it is true, isn't it?"

Todd didn't respond immediately. "It probably is. And even if it isn't all true, I'd heard enough to realize it wasn't wise to let my future be built, or torn down, by a firm that had a bad reputation." He came back and took her into his embrace again. "Besides, I knew I couldn't be involved in the redevelopment of Penny Lane. It would've been a conflict of interests."

That gave Rachel reason to smile—and to reach up and place a quick peck on his mouth. When she drew away, he whispered, "No," and proceeded to kiss her in a most thorough way.

She sighed. "As you were saying, Todd."

"As I was saying, I knew I couldn't work for Silverthorne anymore, even if I wasn't sure about us, about our relationship.'' He ran a hand through his hair. ''After we . . . argued, I began to wonder if I'd been pushing you too hard, overwhelming you with my own certainty that we were right for each other. I also had a few doubts about whether you were totally over Jeff.''

Rachel looked up. ''You don't have doubts now, do you?''

''No,'' he said quietly. ''But at the time I decided I needed some space too. It would be good for me to back away and figure out what was happening between us.''

''And what conclusion did you come to?''

''Only that I couldn't imagine life without you, that it was on-hundred-percent pure misery when I was there and you were here, and I couldn't talk to you or hear your laughter or hold you in my arms.'' As if to emphasize the point, he pulled her closer.

''Why did you go to Seattle?''

''Since I was going to quit Silverthorne, I thought it wise to make contact with my former supervisor. I was seeking some advice, but instead he asked me to come out and talk. It seems the company had just landed another lucrative contract with the city of Seattle. So I flew out and we talked and I was offered my old position back, with assurances that there would be plenty of room for advancement.''

Rachel knew she should be happy for him, congratulate him, but she was stunned by the news. All she could say was, ''When . . . when are you moving back?''

''Next month.'' He took her hands in his, holding her away from him. ''Rachel, I'm willing to move, but not alone. Being with you, all we've been through, changes my perspective on everything. I'd told you I was glad to come home to St. Paul, and I was. But now I know anyplace in the world can be home as long as you're there too.''

"What are you trying to say, Todd?"

"Please come with me. Say you'll marry me. I know how much Cabbage Rose's means to you," he hastened to add. "I would never ask you to give up your boutique. Only change its location. To Nasby Commons."

"The place you said wasn't quite as spectacular as Henley Plaza."

"Yes, but it's still fantastic and it's built on the same concept. There are restaurants, offices, apartments, and, of course, small businesses." His face was a study in earnestness. "Rachel, it would be the perfect spot for an upscale consignment boutique. Several storefronts were vacant when I was there this past week. One of them is waiting for Cabbage Rose."

"You make it sound like a very attractive package deal." Rachel didn't tell Todd that the most attractive part was himself. She longed to say yes, but another obligation weighed on her mind. "I think you know that I love you," she began, "but there's a matter I can't put aside."

"What is it?" He looked worried.

"People I care deeply about, the tenants of Penny Lane, are going to lose their businesses if Silverthorne takes over. I promised I'd do whatever I could. I can't just leave and not help the others fight. There's so much at stake. It's—"

Todd hushed her with a finger to her lips. "There's no need for that. I went by the office to start clearing out my desk. One of the salesmen, who's also quitting Silverthorne, informed me the sale of the Arcade is off. Bradley's in big trouble, and he's pulling out of deals faster than you can say 'sold.' Your friends' businesses are safe."

"Oh, Todd!" No longer tired in the least, Rachel threw her arms around his neck. With surprising energy, he lifted her high in the air and spun her around several times. She laughed exuberantly.

"What will your answer be?" he asked, setting her down at last.

"Yes, I'll marry you, Todd. Yes, I'll live in soggy Seattle and rent a neat little storefront in Nasby Commons. That is, if Cabbage Rose approves," she added playfully.

"Do you think I should ask her in a proper way?" he teased back.

"Of course, but I wouldn't worry too much because she once confided that she'd always wanted to live by the sea."

"Then she will. She'll live in a house where every window looks out on the moody Pacific."

They both knew he wasn't really talking about Cabbage Rose. But as he framed her face in his hands and his mouth sought hers, Rachel believed that whatever promises Todd made, then or forever, he would keep them all.